The Underground

Even the book morphs!
Flip the pages
and check it out!

Look for other **ANIMORPHS**®
titles by K.A. Applegate:

ANIMORPHS®

The Underground

K.A. Applegate

AN
APPLE
PAPERBACK

SCHOLASTIC INC.
New York Toronto London Auckland Sydney

Printed in the U.S.A.

First Scholastic printing, April 1998

For Michael and Jake

CHAPTER 1

My name is Rachel.

You want to know my last name? Too bad. I don't give out my last name. No offense. I'm not trying to be difficult or "too cool." I'm just being careful.

Here's the situation. Earth, our little blue and green planet, the one with the fluffy white clouds and all, is under attack.

It's not under attack like in some World War II documentary or something. Or like in *Star Wars*. It's more subtle than that. Not a lot of explosions and ray guns or whatever. In most wars, I guess what people are after is control of land or territory. Or at least they want to ram some idea down some other person's throat.

1

In this war, our enemies don't care about land. They don't care about ideology. They don't want to take over our capital city and raise some flag or whatever. They want us. They want our physical bodies.

They are called Yeerks. They are a race of parasitic slugs. Like tapeworms or something. They need to live in the bodies of other creatures. Otherwise they're just these gray slugs who slosh around helplessly in a Yeerk pool.

But unlike a tapeworm or something, Yeerks don't live in your intestines. They don't infest your stomach. It's your brain they infest.

They enter through your ear. They can squeeze and flatten themselves out to fit into very small spaces. They enter your ear and then your brain. They squeeze and ooze down into all the little gullies and ridges and folds of your brain. And then they interface with your brain. They control you. Totally, absolutely.

They can open your memories anytime they want. You have no privacy. None. No secrets. None. No escape. None. They are inside your dreams and thoughts and whims and wishes and desires.

Your brain becomes theirs. They own it. They lift your arms and bend your waist. They aim your eyes and focus on what they want to see. They eat for you. They go to the bathroom for you.

And because they have total access to your every single thought, they can pass for you. Flawlessly. They can be you, while always remaining themselves. Your friends will never know. Your mother and father will never know. You will be alone, trapped, helpless, paralyzed in your own body. Unable to make the simplest decision for yourself. Unable to stop yourself when you betray the ones you love. Unable to warn those whom the Yeerks target next.

A Controller. That's what we call a person who has been taken over by a Yeerk. A human-Controller. Although other species around the galaxy have already fallen to the Yeerks.

The Hork-Bajir are enslaved. The Gedds. The Taxxons, although those vile, evil worms did it voluntarily. And we've learned the Yeerks are moving against a race called the Leerans.

And they are moving against Earth, where people live their normal lives never knowing. I guess it's like having cancer or something. You never know the tumor is growing inside you till it's too late.

So now you know why I'm cautious. Why we hide our true identities.

And who are *we*? We are Animorphs. Five kids given the power to morph into any animal we can touch. Five kids who just had the bad luck to be there when the Andalite prince Elfangor landed his damaged ship. Five of us and Elfangor's little brother, the Andalite Aximili-Esgarrouth-Isthill.

We call him Ax.

<Who is this Schwarzenegger?> Ax demanded. <I have heard Marco use his name before.>

"Ah-nuld?" Marco demanded. "Who iss Ah-nuld? Ah-nuld iss der man, zat's who Ah-nuld iss."

<What man?>

"*The* man," Marco explained, explaining nothing.

We were walking through the woods. It was a nice afternoon and school was out for the day. We'd had a half day due to some teacher conference. I don't know what the teachers were conferring about, but it was fine by me. The sun was out. The clouds were fluffy and light, with big sweeps of blue in between. The breeze was warm but not hot. Sitting in school on a day like that would have been a crime.

And since we didn't have anything important to deal with, we were conspiring together to do the thing we were never supposed to do: use our powers for personal, selfish reasons.

But it was tricky, see, because we knew Jake, my cousin and our sort-of leader, might get all tense and righteous on us. Not that he's that way at all. He isn't. But he's very responsible. Some-one has to be, and it sure isn't me.

Still, if he decided to go along with this basi-cally silly idea, we'd do it. If he decided to be against it, we might not do it. Or else Marco and I would do it and not tell Jake.

The trick was to present it the right way.

"See, Jake?" Marco said. "You see how to-tally, pathetically ignorant Ax is when it comes to really important human cultural stuff? Good grief! It makes you want to cry! He knows noth-ing. Nothing! He's been on Earth for months and yet, has he experienced any really important hu-man culture? No. And it's a travesty. A crime. A pity. A shame. It's a —"

"Oh, shu-u-ut up already," Jake interrupted in exasperation. "Let me get this straight. There's a new Planet Hollywood opening in town. And you and Rachel have decided you want to go, but you can't get tickets. So you want to fly there in morph. You want to use our powers for a totally selfish purpose. Is that it, basically?"

I shook my head. "No. Absolutely not. We want to do this for Ax. He needs to be exposed to culture. Me, I don't care." I grinned, unable to lie all that well.

"It's an entertainment event!" Marco cried. "A major, major event. Stars! Famous people!

Millionaires! Babes! A once-in-a-lifetime opportunity for the Ax-man to see Bruce and Demi."

Cassie giggled out loud, then tried to look serious. Tobias, the remaining member of our group, was about a hundred feet above us, floating on a nice warm current of air. He was watching out for any intruders who might get close enough to notice that we were walking around with an Andalite.

In case you've never seen an Andalite, and of course you haven't, they look like a strong blue deer with a mouthless face, with two extra eyes mounted on stalks, weak, human-looking arms, and a vicious scorpionlike tail.

So you can see why we'd want Tobias aloft to keep an eye open. A hawk's eye, no less, which meant no one was going to be sneaking up on us.

Jake nodded at Marco, totally unimpressed. He cocked a skeptical eyebrow at me. "And you figure the human culture Ax needs to be exposed to is Bruce Willis playing a harmonica? Come on, spill it. Why are you into this, Rachel?"

"The whole cultural thing. . . . Okay, look, as part of the deal they're having a fashion show. Ralph Lauren. You know how I feel about Ralph Lauren."

"Oh, man."

"Plus . . ." Marco said, letting the word hang in the air.

"Plus what?" Jake demanded.

I sighed. "Okay, Lucy Lawless is going to be there, too. But that's not why I want to go."

Jake looked puzzled.

"Lucy Lawless," Marco said. "She's the actress who plays Xena: Warrior Princess. Rachel's role model."

Okay, Xena is *not* my role model. That's just some stupid thing Marco made up. He calls me "Xena" to grind my nerves. Marco is good at grinding people's nerves. It's his specialty. If you could get paid for being annoying, Marco would be a millionaire.

But this wasn't the time to slam Marco.

Jake kind of made a face.

"And oh, by the way," Marco said with silky significance, "not that you care, Jake, but a Mr. O'Neal is going to be there. A Mr. Shaquille O'Neal."

"Shaq?"

"Shaq."

"Well, then we're there," Jake said.

CHAPTER 2

We had what should have been the worst tickets at the whole event. We were at least a thousand feet from the main stage. A thousand feet, the length of three football fields plus a little more.

But we could see everything.

I could see flecks of spit when Bruce Willis played his harmonica. I could see Arnold's nose hair. I could see Shaq's shoelaces. I could see the individual buttons on the Ralph Lauren outfits. I could see Naomi Campbell's pores.

And yet she still looked great.

I had the eyes of a bald eagle. And to a bald eagle, a thousand feet is nothing.

I spread my wings six feet wide, stretched out

my wing tips like feathered fingers, and felt the updraft of warm air lift me up and up.

In the air around me, at different altitudes, at various distances, there were a pair of ospreys, a peregrine falcon, a northern harrier, and a red-tailed hawk.

<We look like a raptor convention,> Tobias muttered. <I mean, why not throw in a golden eagle and a few kestrels? If there are any bird-watchers down there, they must be freaking.>

<No one is watching us,> I said. <They're watching Shaq jam with Bruce Willis and John Goodman.>

Tobias is trapped in red-tailed morph. He lives as a red-tail, hunting and killing like a hawk. He has regained his power to morph, even his power to morph into his old human body. But his human body is like any other morph: If he stays in it more than two hours, he'll be trapped in it forever. He'd no longer be able to morph.

The show below us was on a huge outdoor stage. A massive crowd pressed up against the stage, surging and seething and sweating. And not looking all that great, either. I mean, from the air, mostly what you see of humans is their heads. You see little ovals of hair. And let me tell you something: There are a lot of bad haircuts out there.

Planet Hollywood was on the waterfront

where the river cuts through downtown. Tall buildings loomed over it. Skyscrapers fifty and sixty stories tall. I could look right in the windows and see that an awful lot of people had stayed late after work and were gazing down at the stage through binoculars and telescopes.

<There she is!> I yelled in sudden surprise. <I mean . . . oh, that's her. Lucy what's-her-name.>

<Xena! It's Xena!> Marco cried, delighted. <Okay, Rachel, the time has come. Fly down there, morph back to human, and you and Xena have it out. See who can kick whose butt.>

<Marco, Marco, Marco,> I sighed. <You do like to cling to your pathetic little dreams, don't you?>

<Yes. I absolutely do. And Rachel? Don't forget the leather outfit.>

For a moment I considered teaching Marco a lesson. He was in osprey morph. Ospreys are big birds. But they might as well be chickens alongside a bald eagle. It would be so easy to go into a stoop, shoot past him, flare up beneath him, and make him tumble.

Nah. It wouldn't be right.

I wheeled around in a huge circle that carried me close to the Kenny Building. The Kenny Building is one of those glass towers, all smooth and imposing. It sits almost alongside the river, separated from the water by a four-lane road and a strip of grass. The glass is slightly mirrored so normal eyes can't see inside all that well. But bald-eagle eyes are adapted for hunting fish. They see through water very well, and glass is a lot like water.

I saw a man in an otherwise empty office on the next to highest floor. Sixty floors up. I don't know why he caught my eye, but he did. I banked to go back toward him.

And that's when he picked up the metal-framed chair and threw it into the window.

Crash! Glass exploded outward and fell spinning and sparkling to the ground. Big shards sliced through the tops of parked cars.

<What the . . . > I said. <Hey! Guys! Back here! Back here! To the Kenny Building, fast!>

<Is it Arnold?> Marco asked, like that was the only possible reason I could demand his attention.

But Cassie had spotted the crash of the window, too. <Oh, man! That guy is going to jump!>

<I believe he would be injured if he jumped,> Ax observed. <So I doubt he would — Ahh!>

The man had backed up and was running straight for the shattered window.

<There's six of us,> I yelled. <Come on!>

<Not enough,> Tobias said. <But maybe we could make the river.>

11

I raced for the window. The others came flapping up from below, or plunging from above, or wheeling around from the same altitude.

The man ran. He stuck his hands out to push away the last shards of glass. Then he launched himself, feetfirst, into space.

CHAPTER 3

The wind ripped across my face. I used every last ounce of the eagle's flying instincts to gain speed. Was it enough?

I was practically face-to-face with the man as he cleared the building. There was a frozen sort of Road Runner–Wile E. Coyote moment when he seemed to hang suspended in air. Then, he plummeted.

I opened my talons, stretched them forward, and caught a shred of collar as he dropped. Instantly his speed dragged me down and I sank a second talon in. Right around his collarbone. I think I managed to nick him pretty good, but that was the least of this guy's problems.

I opened my wings, but I might as well have

been opening an umbrella. Maybe I shaved one mile an hour off his speed. Not much.

Then Tobias swept in like a guided missile. He grabbed the man's left arm. Jake was next, in his insanely fast peregrine falcon morph. He snagged the back of the man's collar.

He was slowing. But not nearly enough.

<Glide toward the water!> Tobias yelled. <No, don't flap, you idiots, glide!>

I forgave Tobias for calling us idiots. When it comes to flying, he is the expert. And it was a slightly tense situation.

"Aaaaahhhhhhh!" the man screamed so suddenly I nearly lost my grip. He was staring right at me, his left eye maybe an inch from my right eye. He seemed like a normal-looking, middle-aged guy. Aside from the fact that he was screaming in terror.

Cassie and Ax arrived. Both grabbed talon-holds. Marco was last and he went for all that was left, grabbing the back of the man's suit jacket.

<Line up your wings on my angle,> Tobias yelled. <Like you're aiming for a level glide, but stay focused on the river!>

Six birds of prey clutched that man. He screamed. But he was falling slower.

He was definitely falling slower. Still too fast to survive a concrete landing. But slower.

And he was moving forward. Foot by foot, he was moving toward the water's edge.

Down we dropped.

Forward we edged.

I wanted to giggle. It was like some bizarre geometry problem. The sum of the squares of the angles . . . would we make it?

The ground rushed up at us. Cars zipped by at sixty miles an hour below. Then a strip of grass. Way too close! We were no more than fifty feet up.

Water's edge!

<Release!> Tobias cried. <Release, but watch out for the snapback!>

We released. The man dropped. Freed of the weight, I went tumbling, wildly out of control, through the air. I flapped, I spun, I flapped some more, and by a miracle, I righted myself.

Oh. *That's* what Tobias had meant by "snapback."

ZOOOOOM! I blew across the surface of the water, so low my breastbone surfed the tops of the swells.

Wings full again, I caught enough headwind to soar up. <Ah-HAH! Yow! Oh, that was SO cool!> I exulted. Then I felt guilty. <Everyone okay?>

I wheeled around and looked for the man. He was not on the surface of the water. I peered down through the murky, silty river water. The man was ten feet down, waving his arms madly, thrashing and blowing bubbles and looking terrified.

<You have GOT to be kidding,> I moaned. <He's stuck in the mud on the river bottom! Cassie and Marco! Come on, we're supposed to be waterbirds, right?>

I dove straight down into the water.

What a cool feeling. One minute warm air, the next second, cold water.

Then not so cool. The water didn't soak into my feathers, but it did make it impossible to flap my wings. I guess I'd assumed I would sort of fly underwater. Wrong. Eagles may dive and snag fish swimming near the surface, but that does not make them ducks.

<Cassie! Marco! Don't do it!> I yelled in thought-speak.

<No duh,> Marco said. <Just because *you're* a lunatic, doesn't mean we are.>

<Rachel! You have to morph!> Cassie said. <He's struggling!>

I was already changing. Any time you morph, you have to pass through your true body on the way to another form. So there I was, a very wet bird, already feeling my lungs burn, underwater and being swept away by the current.

I morphed as fast as I could. Being terrified always helps.

As soon as I felt my human arms and legs beginning to appear, I fought my way toward the surface. I saw that shimmering, silvery barrier between air and water above me and I used my mutating limbs — feathery, half-bird, half-human stumps — to swim up and up toward air.

I stuck my face up out of the water.

"Aaarrrgghhh!!" someone screamed.

"Oh, my lord, what is it?"

Some people in a little motorboat. I guess they'd been listening to the music from the Planet Hollywood.

I sucked air and went down again.

"I think it was a dead body!"

Thanks, I thought. *I hope that's not a prophecy.*

I focused on morphing a dolphin. I had the DNA inside me, and I'd morphed dolphin before.

Now I was an eerie mix of human and dolphin. Gray rubber skin and legs melted together to make a tail and hands that were turning into flippers.

I powered back toward the poor suicide guy. Although by now I wasn't feeling sorry for him, so much as really annoyed. I mean, what is it with people killing themselves? How big a moron do you have to be not to figure out that at least if you stay alive you have *some* hope, as opposed to being dead and having zero?

Besides, I was missing the fashion show.

He was a weird apparition as he loomed up in front of my dolphin snout. He had sunk up to his thighs in the mud. He'd fought his way partly out, but was still in the goo up to his knees.

And now he was limp, motionless. But I knew he sure wasn't going to die if I could help it, the stupid, inconsiderate jerk.

I buried my snout in the small of his back, bent him backward till he was practically lying on me, and kicked like mad with my dolphin tail.

He came up with a *shloooomp* sound and a cloud of disturbed mud. I pushed him up to the surface and nosed him to the riverbank.

Strong human arms reached for him and yanked him up onto dry land.

Very strong human arms.

CHAPTER 4

"Well, that's just classic," I complained the next day as we all hooked up at the mall food court after school. I had *USA Today*. I had our local newspaper and a bunch of others. Every one of them showed the same picture. And they all had basically the same headline:

**Schwarzenegger Real-Life Hero:
Gives Mouth-to-Mouth to Drowning Man**

One paper said:

Terminator Becomes Resuscitator

"This society is way too celebrity-obsessed," I said. "It is *so* superficial."

"Yeah, I hate that," Cassie said. She gave me a mocking look. Cassie thinks I'm too concerned with looks and clothes. Cassie is my best friend and I would give my life for her, but you should see what she wears. For Cassie, dressing up is putting on *clean* jeans and socks that actually match.

"We were lucky," Jake said. "No one happened to snap any pictures of a pack of raptors carrying the guy to the water. And no one happened to wonder why a dolphin would be so far upstream from the ocean."

"The man was lucky, too," Cassie said.

Marco shook his head. "No way. Lucky would have been getting mouth-to-mouth from Naomi Campbell."

"Where are the cinnamon buns?" Ax asked. "Tobias said he would get some. Cinnamon buns. Bun-zuh."

Ax was there in his human morph, of course, since the sight of an Andalite hanging around the food court would have attracted just a little attention. But the real Ax did not have a mouth. Did not have the ability to make spoken sounds. And worst of all, did not have a sense of taste.

So when he morphed to human, he tended to become fixated on taste and sounds. Especially taste. And especially, ~~~~ on cinnamon buns.

"I wonder what happens ~~~~ now?" Cassie asked.

"Who?"

She rolled her eyes at me. "T~~ man. The man whose life you saved, Ra~

"Oh. Is that his name?"

"Yes, it was in all the newspaper articles," she said, exasperated with me.

I shrugged. "Okay, okay. So his name is George Edelman. Big deal."

Cassie leaned across the table. "Rachel, you saved this man's life. Without you the rest of us wouldn't have seen him in time. Without you he'd have been a splat on the concrete. You are a hero. A human life was saved. He may go on to cure cancer or something. And you don't remember his name?"

Now that she mentioned it, I did feel like maybe I should know the man's name. On the other hand . . . . "Hey, wait a minute. This guy isn't anything to me," I said. "It's not like I'm responsible for him."

Marco made a back and forth gesture with his hand. "I don't know. Isn't it the Chinese who say if you save a man he becomes your responsibility? Or maybe it's the Japanese. The Greeks? Someone. I saw it in a movie."

again. Now I was feeling defen-
was mostly just a goof, you know? I just
anted to see if we could do it. It was . . ." I
searched my mind for the right word. "It was a
challenge. That's it, a challenge."

Tobias arrived, carrying a Cinnabon cinnamon
bun. One of the large ones. Dripping with icing
and smelling of cinnamon. *Lots* of cinnamon.

Ax's human eyes went wide. His mouth hung
open slightly. It was weird, because Ax's human
morph is made up of DNA from Cassie, Jake,
Marco, and me. So you're always seeing something familiar in him, you know? Like maybe it's
your own mouth hanging open, or Marco's eyes.

Tobias set the paper plate down on the table.
"I figured we could all have a bite and then leave
the rest for —" He stopped and stared at Ax with
an expression of amusement mixed with awe.

Ax had snagged the bun. He'd snagged the
plate and the plastic fork, too. He was busy shoving them into his mouth. Bun *and* plate *and* fork.
Great big huge bun and little paper plate.

I reached over and grabbed the end of the
plastic fork. Half of it was already in Ax's mouth.
I yanked it out. It was too late to save the plate.

The five of us just sat there for a few minutes
and watched as Ax chewed and slobbered and
gulped and shoved with his fingertips. It was a

little like watching a python try to swallow a small pig.

"George Edelman, huh?" I said, breaking the spell.

"Yeah," Jake said. "But everyone keep an eye on TV and newspapers for a while, okay? If someone noticed our . . . activities . . . we want to know about it. Mostly, we have to hope George Edelman keeps his mouth shut."

"People will figure he's nuts," Marco pointed out. "No one is gonna listen to a guy who tried to kill himself."

CHAPTER 5

Three days later. My house. My still-not-completely-fixed house.

"Jordan! JORDAN!"

That would be me, yelling. I was in the kitchen. I had opened the refrigerator and discovered that my white paper container of leftover Chinese food was gone.

"Jor-DAN! You little thief."

"What?"

I turned away from the refrigerator and slammed straight into the kitchen island. We didn't used to have a kitchen island. But our kitchen had been annihilated when my bedroom had collapsed down into it.

The construction had been pretty shoddy, I guess. And it hadn't helped at all that I had morphed into an African elephant in my bedroom. Fortunately, no one in my family knew that but me.

Anyway, we were in the process of getting a much cooler kitchen now. My mom's a lawyer and she got the insurance company to pay up right away. Plus the builder of the house was so scared that something else would happen, he was doing all the labor free.

I felt bad about the builder getting blamed. But what was I supposed to say? "Mom, it was me. See, I was allergic to this crocodile morph, and it made me morph out of control so that I . . ." You get the idea. Wasn't going to happen.

Anyway, I slammed into the new kitchen island and fought down the urge to say something I shouldn't repeat. But I was mad, and now I was mad with a bruise on my hip, so I stuck my finger in my little sister's face and said, "You! You ate my Szechuan shrimp! I was saving it. I want it. I want it right now."

A couple years ago that would have scared Jordan. But she's getting older now, and more independent. Plus more of a smart-mouth.

"Rachel, I took your stupid shrimp yesterday. And I threw it out."

"What! You threw out my Szechuan shrimp? You are always doing something with my left-overs."

She shook her head slowly, pityingly. "It was already a week old, *duh*. It was too old, *duh*. It would have made you barf up your kidneys, *duh*. Shrimp doesn't exactly stay good forever, *duh*. And oh, by the way, did I mention, *duh*?"

"You should have asked me!" I cried, in no mood to be reasonable.

"Okay, Rachel," Jordan said placidly. "Should I have thrown out your rancid, bacteria-crawling, moldy leftovers like Mom asked me to, or should I have left them for you to eat so you'd end up having to get your stomach pumped?"

Well. When she put it *that* way. Boy, I hate when someone gets the better of me. But I could not think of a single really crushing comeback. So I said, "I'll let it go this time."

Jordan rolled her eyes. "Thank you, thank you, Queen Rachel. I'm so glad you'll let me live."

My mom walked in, carrying two leather brief-cases. One was normal size. The other was one of those big, kind of square ones. She hefted them both up onto the counter.

She looked tired, like she usually does when she gets home from work. She's not all that high up in the firm, so she works constantly. But she grinned. "Hey! Congratulate me. I'm a celebrity. Did you girls eat? How was school? Where's Sarah? And don't tell me she's at Tisha's house again. Every time she comes home from there I end up buying her another Barbie."

"School was fine," I said. "We haven't had dinner. You want me to make something?"

"Or we could order out," Jordan said smugly. "Rachel would like some pus-oozing, rotten shrimp."

"Mom! Mom!" Sarah yelled, tearing in through the door from the backyard. "Tisha says they have a lawyer Barbie! A lawyer Barbie. Just like you!"

"So what's this about being a celebrity?" I asked.

"Oh, well, I was mostly kidding. You know that guy in the papers a few days ago? The one who was rescued by Arnold Schwarzman? He was on TV and CNN."

"Schwarzenegger?"

"No, the man he rescued. Anyway, guess what? I'm his lawyer. His family says he's incompetent. They want to —"

"Incompetent? Is that where you have to wear those adult diapers?" Jordan asked.

"No, honey, not incontinent. They are alleging he's incompetent. Not able to look after his own affairs. That's what they allege."

"Nuts," I translated. "Wacko. *Allegedly* wacko."

"Don't say wacko," my mother said, looking pained. "Mentally unbalanced will do fine. His family want to have him institutionalized permanently."

"So what are you supposed to do?" I asked. "Prove he's not wacko? I mean, he is, right? He jumped off a building."

"Lawyer Barbie could save him," Sarah said.

"Actually, it's a little worse than that," my mom said, gathering Sarah up into her arms. "Apparently this poor man claims he has an alien living in his head."

My heart beat three times real fast. Then stopped.

"He calls them Yerks or Yorks or something."

CHAPTER 6

"So that's the nuthouse," Marco said with satisfaction as we all gazed up the hill at the pleasant-looking but weirdly quiet two-story structure. "I always suspected I'd end up here."

He gave me a wink. I had to laugh. See, I was about to make that same joke about him. He beat me to it.

Cassie sighed. "I don't think the patients probably like to be called nuts," she said.

"Of course not," I agreed. "They'd have to be nuts to want to be called nuts."

Marco gave me a discreet low five behind my back.

<Cassie's right. It's not politically correct to call nuts nuts,> Tobias said.

Cassie looked at me. "You know, I could swear I heard that bird talking. I must be nuts."

We all laughed. Even Jake, who was trying, with the usual total lack of success, to get us all to behave seriously.

We were gathered near the Rupert J. Kirk State Mental Health Facility. It was two floors of red brick. There was a little fountain just outside the front door, and lots of shade trees and lawn chairs sitting out on the grass. It could have been an old folks' home, or a slightly aged apartment building. Except for the fact that it was encircled by a high chain-link fence. And there were three strands of barbed wire atop that fence. And there was heavy wire mesh on the windows. But aside from all that, it looked perfectly nice.

"Who else has the willies?" Cassie wondered.

I held up my hand.

"What are willies?" Ax asked. He was in human morph.

<A vague, creepy feeling,> Tobias explained. <The subtle, unsettling sense that something you can't quite see is desperately wrong.>

"The feeling I get when I reach the school door every day," Jake muttered.

"School, nuthouse, what's the difference when you get right down to it?" Marco asked philosophically. "Dumb rules and bad food in both places."

Jake jerked his head to indicate we should

move along. We were on the sidewalk across the street, lurking along a row of parked cars. And what's weird is, I swear the sun went behind a cloud the moment we reached the facility.

We walked along, with Tobias flitting from tree to tree overhead.

"Easy enough to bust in," Jake observed. "A fence, a door, big deal. Not like the Fenestre mansion or the Yeerk pool. Easy."

"Yeah," I agreed. "So we get in, we find this George Edelman and try to figure out if he knows something about the Yeerks. Then we leave Marco behind and get out."

Jake raised an eyebrow. "Okay, I think we may have to put a limit on the number of nut jokes. This is serious."

Marco made a deprecating noise. "Nah. This isn't serious."

"Every time we start to take something for granted we end up getting hammered," Jake warned. He grinned in anticipation. "We'd have to be nuts to get careless."

No one laughed.

"I say, we'd have to be *nuts* . . . oh, fine. Don't laugh. I don't care."

"We need an open window or something," I said. I looked over the building. No open windows that I could see. It was thick glass and heavy wire mesh all the way.

31

"We can't hurt anyone," Jake pointed out. "No fighting. Those are innocent people in there. We can't take the risk of hurting anyone. It's too far to travel in fly or cockroach morph. Hmmm. Maybe not that easy, after all."

Just then, like an answer to our prayers, a truck drove up the driveway and around to the far side of the facility.

"Was that a food truck?" Jake asked. "Tobias? Can you go take a look?"

Tobias flapped away and came back in less than a minute. <It's a food delivery. The truck looks pretty big, and it's dark in the back.>

Jake nodded. "Okay, I don't think more than three of us should go. We morph to bird, fly into the truck, morph to human, then to cockroach. We hide in some of the food and they carry us right in. Rachel, this is your guy. I mean, you saved him. So you're in. I'll go. Tobias doesn't have a useful morph, and Ax is too obvious when he passes through his Andalite phase. So it's Marco or Cassie."

We flipped a coin. Marco won. Then we explained to Ax what it meant to flip a coin.

It took twenty minutes for us to find a place to morph into seagulls. Seagulls were less noticeable than birds of prey. Unfortunately, the place we found was a Dumpster. It was an empty Dumpster, but still . . .

As soon as I had my snowy white wings, I was up and out of there. We zoomed around, gaining altitude, and watched as Ax and Cassie retrieved our shoes and outer clothes. We still can't morph regular clothing, just whatever is almost skin-tight. In my case a leotard.

Tobias stayed up at a higher altitude, looking for trouble of any kind.

The three of us waited and watched the back of the grocery truck. There were two guys unloading it. One looked like the driver. The other was wearing a white apron. Probably a cook or something from the facility itself.

<We need to time this right,> Jake said. <I don't want to be a seagull trapped inside a truck.>

<One one thousand, two one thousand, three one thousand . . .> Marco counted off the seconds between trips by the truck driver or white apron guy.

<How about right now?> I said. I spilled air from my wings and dove toward the back of the truck just as the driver went into the building, pushing a dolly loaded with tomato crates.

Jake and Marco fell in beside me and we swooped, swift and neat, into the dark of the truck. I opened my wings and tilted my tail down to kill my speed. Then I took a quick glance around and used my remaining momentum to zip

33

over the top of a wall of cardboard boxes and land in a cramped area behind.

I felt pretty pleased with myself. Marco and Jake landed beside me. Marco landed a little clumsily and sort of rolled and fluttered into the wall of the truck.

<That was dumb, Rachel,> Jake said. <You should have waited.>

<I knew it would work,> I said. I seethed a little at Jake calling me dumb. He wasn't always so careful. Of course, he is our unofficial leader, so I guess he feels responsible. Although as far as I'm concerned, I'm responsible for me.

<Okay, let's demorph,> Jake said. <But this space looks pretty tight back here. So everyone watch your elbows.>

"I'm telling you, I saw some birds fly in here," an irate voice said.

"You see birds? I don't see any birds. Let's get this unloaded. I'm on overtime here, and my company don't pay overtime."

I heard some grunting and the sound of more boxes being lifted. I began to demorph as fast as I could.

CHAPTER 7

Jake was right. It was crowded. We went from being three birds, each smaller than a chicken, to being three kids. We were jammed together, and it wasn't pretty. Marco's hand and fingers were just emerging from his feathers when his arm bones sprouted and forced the fingers into my eyes.

I twisted my head aside as well as I could. But my head was the size of a grapefruit, with my eyes still stuck on the sides and a beak jammed tight into the space between two boxes, so it was hard to move.

There was a pain in my back and I had this jolt of fear. Was I feeling the morphing itself? The Andalite morphing technology keeps that from

35

happening, but was it failing somehow? The pain was pretty severe, like the pressure of a . . . well, of a knee being driven into my back.

<Jake, do you have your knee in —> But just then, thought-speak stopped working as we crossed the line from mostly seagull to mostly human.

In another few seconds we were packed together like sardines in a can. I literally could not move. We were one big mess of knees and elbows and twisted heads.

"This is ridiculous," I muttered.

"Morph to cockroach," Jake managed to whisper.

I've never been crazy about morphing bugs. But this was one case where I was relieved. For once I wanted to get small.

I focused my thoughts on the cockroach. And somehow — I have no idea how — that triggered the cockroach DNA in my system to begin reformulating all the cells in my body.

Of course, a cockroach is minuscule compared to a human being. So I was about to become half as big as my own thumb. According to Ax, all the excess mass gets pushed into Zerospace, where it sort of hangs like a big wad of guts and hair and stuff.

As I morphed the cockroach, as I became smaller and smaller and smaller, more and more of me was being deposited in some blank, white nonspace.

It's not something I like to think about.

In any case, the morphing itself was so disgusting, it distracted me from any such worries.

See, although we were shrinking, we were all still pretty large when the cockroach features began to appear. The extra legs, for example.

Two extra legs sprouted from my chest. They just poked out, like they belonged there. They came out looking like sticks a few inches long. But they just grew and grew and became hairy and articulated. It happened to all of us at almost the same instant.

SPLOOOT!

SPLOOOT!

SPLOOOT!

Unfortunately, we hadn't shrunk to roach size yet. Morphing is never totally logical. Things happen in weird, unpredictable ways. The three of us were each about the size of cocker spaniels when the legs appeared. Followed by insanely long antennae that shot from our foreheads and waved around madly like sensitive bullwhips.

My regular legs were changing. My arms were changing. My face was changing, and that's never good. But it's even worse when you're watching this mirror image of yourself. Marco's smirky face was just six inches from mine when

37

big bug eyes popped out and his lower face split into the creepy, grasping mouthparts of a cockroach.

I've morphed a bunch of times. It is still a freak show nightmare.

The box was getting big beneath me. Now there was so much room I could no longer see Jake at all. Marco was a vague, low-slung shape off across a smooth, light brown cardboard plain.

I tried out my thought-speak. <You guys still there?>

<Yeah,> Jake replied. <Let's take cover inside this box.>

I hadn't really looked at the box to notice what was inside. But I could see an open seam that looked as if it was six feet wide. In reality it was probably an inch. But an inch to a roach is way more space than necessary. A roach can squeeze through a space no wider than the thickness of a nickel.

The final changes were taking place. The hard, fingernail material that made up my outer body replaced the last vestiges of human flesh. The tiny remaining shreds of my liver and heart and lungs all disappeared to be replaced by the utterly primitive organs of the cockroach.

My dim, blurry, distorted roach vision wasn't great, but I was used to it and could more or less make sense out of things as long as they were close. And in addition, I had my antennae. They were tingling with information that seemed like some weird mix of touch and smell. I felt the air currents around me. I felt the vibrations as the cook lifted a heavy load and trudged away. I sensed Marco and Jake, two fellow roaches, although their presence didn't matter much to the roach brain.

But mostly, I smelled food.

Lots and lots of food. Very close by. Sweet. An overpowering smell-touch. Right beneath me.

I powered my six legs and went jerking forward. ZOOM!

It's gross being a roach, but being a *running* roach is amazing. Your face is about a millimeter from the ground. And you feel like you're going two hundred miles an hour. It's as if someone strapped rockets on your back and shot you off across the ground, with your nose practically skinning on the dirt.

I zoomed over to the big seam in the box. Now I could see Marco and Jake fairly clearly. We were all standing next to the edge. We couldn't see down inside and it looked like a big, rectangular well or something.

<What do you think is down there?> Marco wondered.

<I don't know,> I said. <But it's some kind of food, and it smells sweet.>

Suddenly, vibrations. The men were coming back, and I felt a massive, jarring thud as they stuck the edge of the dolly beneath our stack of boxes.

<Let's do it!> I yelled. I powered straight out into the darkness and fell through the perfumed air.

<I hate when she says that,> Marco groaned. <Anytime Rachel says "let's do it" in that insane, suicidal, rock-and-roll way of hers, disaster can't be far away.>

CHAPTER 8

I fell!

Down and down and down. Probably at least three inches.

I hit bottom, only bottom wasn't flat. It was curved and pitched. I grabbed with the tiny claws at the ends of my legs, but I slipped farther before I could latch on.

Jake and Marco dropped not far away.

I looked around as well as I could in the gloom. I was standing on something almost cylindrical, except that it was also curved. And pressed in right beside this curved cylinder was another, each maybe ten times my own body length. And wait! Others, all around. In addition

41

to being cylindrical and curved, now I could see that they tapered down to a blunt tip.

Some of these curved things were gathered together at one end, like a bunch of . . .

<Bananas,> Marco said. <We're in a crate of bananas.>

<Oh. That must be what we were smelling. The sweet smell,> Jake said. <Good. This should be easy. They're moving us now. In a few seconds we'll be inside.>

<Gross. Roaches on bananas,> I said, making conversation while we waited. <Maybe that's why Cassie always washes her bananas before she peels them.>

<No,> Jake said. <It's because of pesticides. You know, poisons.>

<Poison?> Marco said nervously. <I don't feel sick. At least, I don't think I feel sick.>

<It would just be trace amounts,> Jake said. <But I suppose they spray poison on the bananas down in wherever. Ecuador or wherever.>

<Ecuador? That just popped into your head? Ecuador?> Marco demanded. <Besides, Cassie's probably wrong. What's going to eat through banana skin? This skin is like foot-thick leather.>

<I think it's for the spiders,> I said. <Haven't you ever heard how sometimes there are tarantulas crawling around bananas? Happens all the

time. They come up in the holds of ships and —>

<Excuse me? Tarantulas?> Marco squeaked.

<Oh, come on. What are the odds that there's a tarantula in this particular crate of bananas?>

Unfortunately, right at that moment I got the answer. The crate was out of the truck and a bright beam of sunlight shone down through the opening in the box. A brilliant shaft illuminated the bananas. It was a bizarre landscape. Curves everywhere. Like someone with a protractor had drawn an endless jumble of arcs.

It was about eight inches away. Sitting comfortably atop a bunch of bananas. It was, no exaggeration, as big as an elephant to me.

<Um, guys? Don't anyone make any sudden movements, okay?>

<Oh, puh-leeze,> Marco said. <How lame do you think we are, Rachel? Now you're going to pretend there's a tarantula in here? So I'm supposed to go screaming around like a nitwit while you laugh yourself sick?>

<Marco. Jake. Just look behind you.>

I guess they looked.

<Aaaaahhhh!>

<Aaaaahhhh!>

They ran. The spider moved.

Roaches are fast. Tarantulas are faster.

I would have never believed something that big could move that fast. But I guess it had been a long, hungry boat ride up from Ecuador for the tarantula.

<Rachel! Where are you?> Jake yelled.

Eight hairy legs were a blur. All I could focus on was a huge, ripping beak like a hawk's, and eight eerie eyes all in a cluster in that huge hairy face.

It was after me!

I motored. I leaped as well as my roach legs could leap. In some tiny corner of my tiny roach brain I heard the cockroach instincts screaming, *Fly! Fly!*

I fluttered open the hard shell that covered my gossamer roach wings and I flew. I flew nowhere! Maybe two inches! Roaches can't fly worth a —

It was on me! Looming over me! The sunlight streamed down and then a shadow. Not the shadow of the spider, something bigger, farther away.

I was looking up at nostril! A pair of huge, hairy, human nostrils. And beyond them, weirdly bright human eyes.

I tried to run, but the spider reared up, flailing its front legs like a frightened horse. It jammed one of those legs down so fast I didn't see it move. A claw grabbed my left middle leg. I fought and twisted, but there was no escape.

Huge fangs were descending on me.

Then, "Oh! Oh! Aaaarrrggghh! A spider!"

Everything went nuts. The bananas went flying. We were falling, me and the tarantula, which still refused to let me go. Monstrous bananas, each as big as a piece of concrete sewer pipe, fell toward us. But the spider and I were falling, too.

WHAM!

Bananas all over me. Brilliant sunlight everywhere!

In panic, the cook had knocked the pile of boxes off his dolly. The banana crate had smashed down onto the floor just inside the loading dock.

"What are you doing with my bananas?" the truck driver yelled. Then, "Oh, jeez! Kill it!"

I'd been battered and beaten by falling bananas, but that spider still had me. And now, in addition to the sheer, screaming panic I felt, the roach brain was adding the terror of sudden, bright light.

Run! the roach brain yammered.

Run! my brain agreed.

"Stomp it!" someone yelled in a voice that vibrated down through my body.

A huge, slow-moving shadow came down and down and down.

SQUISH! A banana exploded under the impact of the giant shoe. It gushed banana goo, sweet and sticky, all over us.

And still that tarantula held me. Eight huge, expressionless black eyes glared down. The gnashing, hungry beak strained for the chance to rip me open.

<Is that one of you?> Tobias cried from far away.

Thanks be to a million years of evolution that has given the hawk its magnificent eyes. Oh, yes, oh, yes, love those eyes.

<It's me!> I yelled.

I didn't see Tobias come falling from the sky. All I saw was a blur of big, craggy talons snatch the spider up, up and away.

I kept my grip on a banana. My leg was ripped away by the spider, which flatly refused to let go. It hurt in a sort of vague, distant kind of way. But roaches are pretty tough.

<Let's move!> Jake said. <Head toward the shade. That should be the inside of the building.>

We moved out. I moved a little more slowly, and with a tendency to drift toward the side with the missing leg.

And from high above I heard Tobias say, <Hmmm. Not bad. Not bad at all.>

<See, this is what happens whenever Rachel starts in with her "let's do it" attitude,> Marco complained as we scurried across a filthy floor. <We end up being eaten by spiders or something.>

<Hey, I don't see where *you* suffered, Marco,> I said. <I'm the one who can only count to five on her legs.>

<Stick close to the base of the wall,> Jake said. <I don't want to get stomped. I got swatted in fly morph, and that's enough for me. I am not getting stomped on, too.>

We were a little shaky, obviously.

<You think Tobias actually ate that spider?> Marco asked.

47

<With banana relish,> I said.

We laughed a nervous kind of laugh and continued zooming along the rubber baseboard in the facility's kitchen. Then, an opening in the wall and we were in. I was grateful to be out of the harsh light. And away from so many shoes.

<I've spotted the guy.> It was Cassie's thought-speak voice.

I was puzzled. <What are you doing?>

<Ax and I morphed to harrier and osprey. We've been looking in the windows, trying to spot Mr. Edelman. I have him. Second floor. Above the kitchen, then maybe twenty feet along the building. He's in a room with three other patients. They're wearing hospital gowns and slippers. They're watching TV.>

<It's the show called *Gilligan's Island*,> Ax added helpfully.

<Now, how does Ax know about *Gilligan's Island*?> Marco wondered. No one answered him.

<Okay, straight up,> Jake said.

The inside of the wall was a natural home to cockroaches. In fact, I noted several scattered areas of roach poop.

It's the kind of thing a roach brain notices.

The inside of the wall was otherwise a pretty clean place. I was standing on a wide expanse of wood. The grain was like ripples under my roach feet. A nail head protruded in front of me and looked about as tall as a tall woman. To my left and right were the backsides of Sheetrock — featureless, blank, gray.

We tried our feet out on the Sheetrock. They tended to slip. So we scuttled down to an upright beam and climbed the wood instead.

Eight feet straight up, and it was weirdly like flying. I felt the "ground" recede way, way below me. Dozens of times my own height. I knew I wouldn't be hurt if I fell. But still, hanging sideways, crawling straight up against gravity, seemed dangerous.

We reached the top of the beam and I was grateful to haul myself up and over into a space between the upright and a cross beam. We were just beneath the floor. But now things were complicated. The space between the second floor and the ceiling beneath it was mostly blocked by a wall of wood. But eventually we found a way in, walking sideways and scraping between rough-sawed wood-ends.

My antennae waved wildly, trying to comprehend the long, square tunnel before me. It was almost pitch-dark. Only a tiny hint of light filtered down from the floor above. And after the run-in with the spider, I was very jumpy. Who knew what might be in that vast, dark space?

<That light must be from some kind of

crack,> Jake said. <I guess we go toward that. Unless anyone else has any ideas?>

<I have an idea,> Marco said. <We get out of here, go back to the mall, and see how many Cinnabons Ax can eat before he explodes.>

<Oh, come on, you babies,> I said, trying to sound braver than I felt. <Let's go.> I scuttled forward. I was walking on Sheetrock that formed the ceiling below. The wooden walls on either side of me were insanely tall — ten, twenty times my height.

But we soon reached the light. I felt better. My roach brain felt worse. Across our path lay a huge tube. It seemed to be metal and looked as big as a felled redwood. From the large tube, two smaller tubes went straight up toward a brighter light.

<Plumbing,> Jake remarked.

Sudden movement in the darkness!

<Aaahhh!> I yelled, but even as I was yelling, I realized what it was.

<A brother roach,> Marco said. <Or sister.>

<Come on, let's get this over with,> I said. I scampered straight up the nearest vertical pipe. And within seconds I was poking my bullwhip antennae out into the light beneath a sink.

<It's a bathroom,> I reported. <Come on.>

We piled out through the hole, and down onto cold, white ceramic tile.

<Are we in the right place?> Marco wondered.

<I don't know. I forgot to bring my map of the inside of the walls of the nuthouse,> I said. <We need to have Cassie or one of the guys confirm where we are. There's a window up there.>

I took off, scurrying across the tile, up the wall and onto the wire mesh of the window. I could see light, of course, but could not see through the glass.

<Hey, Cassie, Ax, Tobias. Do you see a roach sitting on a window?>

Ax answered. <Yes. I see you. You are in a small room just alongside the room where the human named Edelman is.>

<Thanks.> I rejoined the others. <So. Now what?>

<Now we talk to Mr. Edelman,> Jake said. <We need to get him to come in here. We'll have some privacy in here.>

<And then what, he talks to a cockroach?>

<No. One of us needs to demorph and talk to him,> Jake said.

<Wait a minute,> Marco objected. <Isn't he going to think it's a little weird, some kid appearing magically in his bathroom?>

<It's a facility for people with mental illnesses, Marco,> Jake pointed out. <Who's going to believe him?>

<I'll do the talking,> I said. <Mr. Edelman is

51

my responsibility. I rescued him. And I'm starting to think I'm sorry I did. You guys stay out of the way. I'd hate to accidentally step on you.>

I began to demorph.

The squares of ceramic tile grew rapidly smaller. I shot up and up, like Jack's magic bean sprout or something.

I was about two feet tall, with skin like burnt sugar, monstrously long antennae sprouting from my forehead, human eyes, semihuman legs that bristled with dagger-sharp hairs, blond hair, and a wide, throbbing yellowish-brown abdomen, when the bathroom door opened.

A man shuffled in, wearing slippers. He headed for the toilet. He hesitated. Slowly, very slowly, he turned.

My human mouth was just appearing. My lips grew from melted roach mouthparts.

"Hi. Could you get George Edelman for me?"

The man nodded. "Sure." He started to go. Then he turned back. "Are you real?"

"Nah. Just a figment of your imagination."

"Ah. I'll get George."

CHAPTER 10

I was human by the time Mr. Edelman poked his head cautiously into the room.

"Hi," I said cheerfully. I stuck out my hand. "I'm . . . I'm helping your lawyer with your court case."

He was startled. Who wouldn't be? He swept his eyes around the room as though maybe, just maybe, there was something weird about meeting me in a bathroom. He didn't notice the two cockroaches huddled together under the sink.

"Who are you? What are you doing here?" Then he looked down. "You're not wearing shoes."

"Yes, I apologize for my slightly . . ." I was looking for a sophisticated word like "unconventional," but I couldn't think of it. ". . . my slightly weird appearance here."

"Yes. Weird." He glared at me for a while, uncertain what to make of my utterly bizarre appearance in his bathroom. Then he shook my outstretched hand. "I guess I'm not one to be talking about 'weird.'"

"Would you like to have a seat?" I said, indicating the toilet.

"No. Thanks." Again the look that said, "Wait a minute, I may be nuts, but there's something strange about this." Then he said, "You're awfully young."

"Thank you," I said. "Actually I'm twenty-five, but I work out, I eat the right foods, and I always wear sunscreen. Mr. Edelman," I said bluntly, before he could ask me any more questions, "why did you try to kill yourself?"

He sat down on the edge of the tub. I leaned against the sink and tried to look like a very youthful twenty-five-year-old with no shoes. Mr. Edelman looked at me with confused, but kind, gray eyes. He made an effort to smooth his rumpled hair.

And he said, "I had no choice. It's this thing in my head."

I nodded. "Okay. Yes. What thing in your head?"

"The Yeerk." He made a weak smile, like he

was expecting me to laugh and denounce him as a lunatic.

My heart beat faster and I missed a breath. I sucked in a lungful and kept my expression fixed.

"What exactly is a Yeerk, sir?"

He hesitated again. He was tired of telling stories no one believed. Maybe he was on prescription drugs. They do that in psychiatric hospitals. He was probably loaded up on tranquilizers or something. All of a sudden, I felt sorry for him.

"Mr. Edelman, I promise you I won't laugh. And I won't make you take any pills. And I won't say you're crazy. Can you tell me what you mean when you say 'Yeerk'?"

He nodded. "Yes. Yeerks are parasitic aliens. They enter the brain through the ear canal. They take over every function of your conscious mind. They . . ." Suddenly he went into a spasm. It wracked his body. He jerked wildly, wrapped his arms tight together, and tried to control it. His mouth snapped open and shut like some mad ventriloquist's dummy.

I grabbed him by the shoulders, trying to do something to help. But then he started raving. He was speaking in a strange, manic voice.

"I I I what? *Farum yeft kalash sip! Sip! Sip!* The pool! *Gahala sulp!* AAAAHHH! Help! *Coranch! Coranch!*"

Suddenly, he fell silent and almost collapsed. I propped him back up.

"Are you okay?"

"No," he whispered. "It happens sometimes. It's the Yeerk. You see, he's mad. Insane. He's in my head and he won't get out. But he is insane! Insane!"

"Okay, okay, try and chill, okay, Mr. Edelman?"

"Yes. Yes."

"Look, I can't stay much longer. But you have to tell me: How is the Yeerk staying alive without Kandrona rays? You've been in here for more than three days."

I cannot possibly describe the way he looked at me then. Hope. Dread. Amazement. All three.

I grabbed him again by the shoulders. "I know it's weird, but you have to trust me. How does it happen? Why is the Yeerk insane? How does it survive without the Kandrona?"

"Andalite?" Mr. Edelman whispered wonderingly.

"Yes," I lied. "Andalite."

"It's the food," he said, gushing the information. "The food! During the famine after . . . after you Andalites destroyed the one Kandrona, we found out, *they* found out that a certain food could help them get by. For a while. But there were problems with it — AAHHH! *Yeft, hiyi yarg felorka! Ghafrash fit Visser!*"

Mr. Edelman jerked and slavered and yelled for a few minutes and I waited and worried that someone might come. Some attendant or doctor or something. But no one did.

I wished I could help the man. I had spent enough time close to Controllers of various types — human, Hork-Bajir, and Taxxon — to guess that some of what he was saying was in the basic Yeerk language. And other words were Hork-Bajir. Yeerks seem to adopt some of the language of their hosts. The Yeerk who was in Edelman's head must have been a Hork-Bajir-Controller at one point.

Mr. Edelman calmed down and got control of himself again. "Sorry. The Yeerk breaks through sometimes. What you hear is the raving of a crazy Yeerk."

"It's okay," I said. "What's this food? The food that allows Yeerks to survive without the Kandrona?"

"They discovered it quite by accident. No one guessed what it could do. No one realized it would prove addictive. But it did. Terribly addictive. And over time, the continued ingestion of it began to eliminate the Yeerks' need for Kandrona rays. At the same time, it drove them crazy. You see, it seems to literally replace some of a Yeerk's brain stem."

I nodded. I could barely contain my excitement. A food that could destroy Yeerks! "What is the food, Mr. Edelman?"

"Oatmeal," he said. "But only the instant kind. And then, only the maple and ginger flavor." He shook his head. "Yeerks cannot resist the addiction, once exposed. And they slowly, but surely, drive themselves mad. There are dozens of men and women like me. In places like this. On the streets. Or worse."

"Thanks for telling me," I said. "Um . . . Listen, is there anything I can do for you?"

He shook his head a little sadly. "The Yeerks will leave me alone. After all, who is going to believe a madman? I . . . I am sorry I tried to destroy myself. It all just got to be too much. This . . . this alien lunatic in my head. My family wanting to keep me locked up in here."

"Isn't there some way to get the Yeerk out of your head?"

"No. No. He will live as long as I do."

I've never seen sadder eyes. I hope I never see eyes that sad again. I looked away.

"I just wish . . . the times when I am myself, when I am in control, I wish I didn't have to spend them in here."

He looked out through the dirty bathroom window with its heavy wire mesh.

CHAPTER 11

"We have our ultimate weapon," Marco reported to the others when we were all safely assembled back in Cassie's barn. "Maple and ginger oatmeal."

"*Instant* maple and ginger oatmeal," I corrected.

"Instant," Marco agreed.

Cassie, Ax, and Tobias all just stared. Tobias was his hawk self, and he can really stare. Ax was in his own Andalite body, and he could stare with four eyes at once.

"Oatmeal," Cassie said.

"Oatmeal," Jake confirmed. "But only the instant maple and ginger. I guess they don't know why."

<Maybe it's the maple,> Tobias suggested.

"Maybe it's the ginger. Or maybe it's the 'instant.' Whatever that is," I said. "Who cares? Suddenly we have a weapon to use on human-Controllers. A human-Controller who eats this stuff gets hooked and the Yeerk in his head goes nuts. What we have to do is find some way to get a lot of this stuff into a lot of Controllers."

I took a sidelong glance at Cassie. Something told me she was not going to approve of this. But Cassie was bending over a cage, poking her fingers through the wire to check a bandage on an injured badger.

To my surprise, it was Tobias who said, <You know, something about this doesn't feel totally okay. You know?>

Marco, who had been lounging on a bale of hay, jumped up. "What? What? We have green kryptonite here! We have something that can make Yeerks go nuts. Why is that not a good thing?"

<It sounds to me like they get addicted to it. Like a drug,> Tobias said.

I winced. "It's oatmeal, okay? Not anything illegal."

<A drug is in the eye of the beholder,> Tobias argued. <If you get addicted to the illegal stuff and it messes you up, that's a drug to you. If you get addicted to oatmeal and it messes you up —>

"It's still just oatmeal," I said. "Oatmeal is oatmeal. Jeez! I can't believe we're having this conversation."

"Look," Marco said, "the bigger question here is WHO CARES?! They're Yeerks. They're the enemy. They attacked us, not the other way around."

<What about the hosts? The humans?> Ax asked. <The Yeerks are made invulnerable to their normal hunger for Kandrona rays. They can live inside their human hosts forever, even if the oatmeal is later taken away. These hosts would lose all hope.>

"If we lose this war we're all going to be without hope," I said. "Ax, I can't believe you, of all people, would even hesitate."

Ax swiveled his stalk eyes toward me. <We Andalites have been at war longer than you. We understand the temptation to sink to the level of your enemy.>

"Sink to the level of —" I started to yell.

Ax cut me off. <We also know that you can't win if you are not prepared to be a little ruthless. It's a question of balance. How far into savagery do you go to defeat the savage?>

I looked around the barn. Marco and I had drawn closer, almost unconsciously. Tobias was up in the rafters, using his hawk senses to listen and look for anyone approaching the barn. Ax was shifting on his four legs and stretching his scorpionlike tail.

Jake and Cassie were the only ones not to say much. Jake looked troubled. He was staring, but not at anything real. I could guess his thoughts. His brother, Tom, is a Controller.

But it was Cassie who surprised me. Usually she's the one getting all moral.

"Cassie?" I asked. "What do *you* think?"

She hesitated. Like she just wanted to keep tending to the badger. She sighed and stood up. When she turned around, I was shocked. She had a stricken look.

"I . . . I don't know anymore, okay?" she said.

I was confused for a moment. Then it hit me. We'd had a bad run-in with a human-Controller whose Yeerk was Visser Three's twin brother. This Yeerk had found another way around the Kandrona. He cannibalized fellow Yeerks. Sometimes human hosts got in the way.

In the heat of the moment, hearing that evil creature speak, Cassie had demanded his destruction. She'd asked Jake to do it. Jake had refused.

I don't know why, but it frightened me to think of Cassie not knowing what was right and wrong. Or at least thinking she didn't know. Cassie was my best friend. I counted on her to balance me. She was supposed to be sensible when I was reckless. She was supposed to be moral when I was ruthless.

But things had gotten more and more confused for all of us, I guess.

"Look," I said, "okay, maybe this oatmeal is a drug to the Yeerks. But you know what? This is a war. Sooner or later, if we are successful, if the Andalites send help, if the human race rises up, we're going to try and destroy every Yeerk on planet Earth. Right? That's our goal. This isn't like some normal war where you hope you can make peace and compromise. We can't compromise. The Yeerks are parasites. How do we compromise? Let them have a few million humans as hosts?"

<They will never compromise, anyway,> Ax said. <They must be forced back to their own home world.>

<So we try and feed them addictive drugs,> Tobias said with obvious distaste.

"It's OAT-freaking-MEAL!" Marco exploded.

Cassie suddenly laughed. It was a cynical laugh. I didn't know she was capable of a cynical laugh. "And all the rights and wrongs, and all the lines between good and evil, just go wafting and waving and swirling around, don't they?"

Jake shook off his funk and stepped to the center of our little group. "I have to ask myself: If it were Tom, and it may be Tom in the end, would

I do this to him? On the one hand, life as a slave of a Yeerk. No free will at all. On the other hand, as we saw with Mr. Edelman, some free will, some ability to communicate, but with this insane Yeerk in your brain."

<So?> Tobias asked him. <What's your answer?>

Jake shrugged. "In the Civil War, they were ending slavery. Most of the Southern soldiers who were killed weren't slave owners. They were just guys trying to be brave. Maybe they could have worked out a compromise. Maybe they could have ended the war earlier if the North had agreed to leave some people as slaves. But would that have been right? No. So the war had to go on till *everyone* was free."

<Or dead,> Tobias added grimly. <But okay, that's a pretty good example. You're right. I hate it, but you're right. We have to win.>

I laughed without any humor at all. I'm pretty gung ho. Unlike Cassie, unlike Tobias perhaps, I'm ruthless at times. But even I have enough sense to know the words "we have to win" are the first four steps on the road to hell.

And I noticed that Jake never answered himself about his brother. Would Tom be getting the magic oatmeal slipped into his breakfast?

Not a chance. Jake still hoped to rescue Tom some day. And from what Edelman had said, there was no rescue from an oatmeal-altered Yeerk.

"Where do we find a bunch of human-Controllers sitting down to eat?" Marco wondered.

I sighed. "The Yeerk pool, Marco. The Yeerk pool."

CHAPTER 12

The Yeerk pool. I dreamed about it that night.

I didn't use to dream much. Or at least, I seldom recalled my dreams. I dream a lot now. Terrible dreams where I'm trapped in some hideous shape, half-human, half-insect. I dream about that awful battle in the ant tunnels. I dream about the screaming, slashing massacre when we took the Kandrona at the top of the EGS Tower.

But I dream most about the Yeerk pool. I hear the screams and curses of human hosts held in cages while their Yeerks swim in the leaden water of the pool. I hate that sound. I hate the sound of despair. It makes me mad. In my dream I'm mad at those poor people and I want to yell, "Why don't you fight? Why don't you fight?"

But then it's me. It's me being led out onto that steel pier by a pair of Hork-Bajir warriors. It's me kicking and screaming and begging, "Please, please, someone help me!" Knowing there is no help.

Knowing I am doomed, and feeling the despair, and hating that feeling inside of me.

I feel the Hork-Bajir kick my legs from under me. And I'm facedown on the steel pier. And they shove me forward till my face is just an inch above the gray sludge of the Yeerk pool.

It seethes and boils with the swift movements of the Yeerk slugs.

And then my head goes down. Down into the liquid. And the Yeerk that will own me is there. I see him, a gray slug, a vague, indistinct shape in the liquid.

I struggle, but what can I do against two Hork-Bajir? I struggle, but my head is held there as I scream bubbles.

The Yeerk touches my ear. Like a large snail. That's how it feels. Then the pain . . . it forces its way into my ear! It's inside my ear! The pain is incredible, but so much worse is simply knowing it has me.

It surges into my brain.

And I am yanked, gasping, up from the pool.

I try to grab my ear. But my arm no longer works.

I try to yell. But my mouth is not mine anymore.

So I scream, in some dark, lonely corner of my own brain, I scream.

And the Yeerk chuckles as it opens my memories and reads my life. And I give way to the despair.

When I woke up I had soaked the pillow with my sweat. I stared at the clock. Three-twenty-seven. A.M.

The Yeerk pool. We were going back to the Yeerk pool. And I, Rachel, mighty Xena, fearless, pulled the covers up over my head and shook.

At dawn I got up and put on a robe. It was cloudy out, so the dawn was just gray. But I went to my window and opened it, just as I do every morning.

Tobias arrived, almost silent. He swept inside and landed easily on my dresser.

<How you doing?> he asked.

"Fine," I whispered. "How about you?"

I have to whisper when Tobias comes over. My sisters are right in the next room. I keep my door locked.

<I had a nice breakfast,> Tobias said. <A lucky hunt.>

I went to my desk and opened my book. It was my homework. "Can you stand math?"

<I've gotten so I kind of like math,> Tobias said. <It's something that's the same for all humans or whatever.>

I opened my book.

I guess it was a weird scene. Me, with this big red-tailed hawk perched on the edge of my desk. Sitting there in the glow of a single lamp, while the rest of my family still slept. But we did it lots of mornings. Whenever Tobias managed to find an early breakfast and it wasn't raining.

<You worried about going back to the Yeerk pool?>

I laughed nonchalantly. "If I'm ever *not* worried about going to the Yeerk pool, you can lock me up with Mr. Edelman."

<Yeah. Look, I'm going with you guys this time. What morph do you think we'll use?>

I sighed. "You don't have to do this, you know."

<Yes I do. What morph?>

"I don't know. Probably fly or cockroach. Do you have an entrance for us?"

Part of what Tobias did with his long days, while the rest of us were in school, was monitor the movements of known Controllers. He kept track of the ever-shifting entrances to the Yeerk pool. It was fairly easy for him.

<Yeah, I have an entrance,> he said. If he'd had a mouth, he would have grinned. <You guys are going to love this one.>

I gave him a sidelong look. "If it leads to the Yeerk pool, I don't think I'll ever love it."

CHAPTER 13

<This was not easy to figure out,> Tobias said proudly. <Hours and hours of following known Controllers. Then I had to keep stealing peeks in through the windows. I even morphed to human to check out the inside. That's how I found out about the Happy Meal.>

We were flies. The six of us. We were inside a McDonald's, zipping madly around. It was crazy. The scent of food was everywhere. Pickles. Meat. Ketchup. Grease. Special sauce.

My fly body thought it had died and gone to heaven. Outside of a good trash dump, there's no place a fly likes more than a fast-food restaurant.

<What about the Happy Meal?> Cassie asked.

<Why is the meal happy?> Ax asked.

Tobias decided to answer Cassie's question. <That's how you signal. That's the code. You go up to the counter and say "I'd like a Happy Meal. With extra happy." That's the signal.>

I flew upside down along the ceiling, looking for a place to land and rest. I buzzed to a nice greasy patch near the deep fryer, turned a back flip, and set down. My mouth — actually, it was more like some insanely long straw that could curl up — extended down and began spitting digestive juices onto the grease, then sucking up the resulting goo.

Hey, I know it's gross. But it was either that or keep resisting the fly's desperate cries for food! food! food!

<After you place the Happy Meal order, you go around like you're going to the bathroom. But instead, you take the other door. The one that goes to the kitchen. You go in — and here's the cool part — you go into the walk-in refrigerator.>

<Then what?> Jake asked.

<Then I don't know. I could never see all the way inside.>

<Okay. So here's the plan,> Jake said. <We watch till someone orders the Happy Meal with . . . what was it?>

<Extra happy,> Tobias said.

<Is it just my imagination, or did the Yeerks develop a sense of humor?> Marco asked.

<Once we have our Controller, we follow him in. No problem,> Jake said. Then he added grimly, <Oh yeah, no problem. A little picnic in the Yeerk pool. I'm sure they'll all buy that.>

<Um, Jake?> Marco said. <You said that last part out loud. We heard it.>

<Oh. Sorry.>

<Mr. Inspiration,> I said with a laugh. <Come on. Let's —>

<Uh-uh-uh! Don't say "let's do it," Rachel,> Marco yelled.

We took turns hanging out above the counter. But we didn't have too long a wait till a woman came in and ordered a Happy Meal with "extra happy."

We buzzed easily along behind her as she went through the door and into the kitchen. Then into the walk-in refrigerator.

<Gotta get out of here, man,> I said. <This cold is slowing me down.>

<Yes, this body has no ability to regulate body temperature,> Ax observed. <What a strange idea. You humans do many unusual things.>

<Ax, I don't think we're exactly responsible for —>

<Yes, I know. I was attempting to make a joke. A human-style joke.>

<Great,> Marco muttered. <Funny Yeerks and now a wannabe-funny Andalite.>

The Controller woman waited patiently and after a few seconds, the back of the walk-in refrigerator split and opened wide.

She stepped and we flew through the opening. It really was going to be easy this time.

BrrrrEEEEET! BrrrrEEEEET! "Unauthorized life-form detected." BrrrrEEEEET BrrrrEEEEET! "Unauthorized life-form detected."

The Controller woman looked around. I saw her blue eyes, each the size of a swimming pool, turn and look. Through the shattered, splintered fly vision, I could see her focus.

Then she muttered under her breath, "Security fanatics. It's just a couple of lousy flies."

But the mechanical voice was giving instructions now.

"Shut your eyes tightly to protect against retinal damage from the Gleet BioFilter."

<The what?> I asked.

<Get out of here!> Ax yelled.

<What?>

<Out! Out! Out!> he yelled.

Ax never yells. So if he does yell, you have to figure it's a good idea to pay attention.

I spun around in midair the way only a fly can do, and I hauled wing for the still-open crack that led to the refrigerator.

Suddenly, the whole world blew up in a dazzling explosion of light. I felt my compound eyes melt. I flew on, blinded, blew through the rapidly narrowing crack and hit the cold air.

<I'm blind!> I cried.

<I think we all are,> Ax said calmly. <We're lucky to be just blinded. A Gleet BioFilter destroys all life-forms whose DNA is not entered into the computer controls. Andalite technology, of course. The Yeerks must have stolen the specifications.>

<Ax, are you telling me that filter thing will wipe out any life-form except the one they program it for?> Jake asked.

<Yes, Prince Jake. I'm sorry to say, yes. Everything but the particular human-Controller.>

<Then we're shut off from the Yeerk pool,> Tobias said. <They must have this same technology at all the entrances now.>

It was hard to get *too* upset by the idea of being locked out of the Yeerk pool. But it was frustrating. And it kind of made me mad. I didn't like the idea of being outsmarted by the Yeerks.

<There must be some other way in,> I said.

<I'd like to know what it would be,> Marco said.

For a moment no one said anything. Then Cassie said, <Well . . . there is one way.>

<I take it back!> Marco said. <I take it back! I can tell by your tone, Cassie, I really *don't* want to know.>

CHAPTER 14

Back at Cassie's barn we gathered around and stared at a small cage.

"What is that, a rat?" Marco asked.

<It's a mole,> Tobias said.

"Count on Tobias to know his rodents," Marco said. He looked up at the rafters where Tobias was preening — cleaning his feathers with his beak. "How do they taste?"

<I've never caught one. They don't come up to the surface very often.>

"That is one ugly creature," I said. "And it looks way too much like a shrew." I had morphed a shrew once. It wasn't a good time. The shrew was way too hyped. Way too excitable. And way, way too hungry.

"It's a lot calmer than a shrew," Cassie said. "And like Tobias said, moles spend almost all their time underground. They dig tunnels. See how big the front feet are? They're well-adapted for digging tunnels."

Marco sighed. "*Moleman*. You can't even picture a superhero named *Moleman*. What would the superpowers be? Digging?"

<Many of your Earth animals are similar to this in shape,> Ax observed.

"Yeah," Cassie agreed. "It's a very successful shape: rats, mice, voles, shrews, even squirrels and raccoons to a certain extent. Your basic low-slung, four-legged rodent shape."

I sighed. "So let me get this straight. You're suggesting we morph this mole and *dig* our way down to the Yeerk pool?"

Cassie shrugged. Then she winked at me. "Just trying to be helpful."

"It's probably, what, fifty feet down through the dirt to the top of the Yeerk pool?"

<At least,> Tobias said.

"That's a lot of dirt," Jake said. "But I don't know of another way. If we're going to do this, we need to get back to the Yeerk pool."

"Has anyone figured out how we're supposed to get a whole lot of oatmeal down there after we dig these mole tunnels?" I asked.

Jake nodded like he was going to say "sure."

Instead he said, "Nope. But we need to start stocking up. Everyone start bugging your parents to buy instant maple-and-ginger flavor oatmeal. Lots of it. We'll start with that. Then we'll spend our allowances for more."

Marco shook his head. "No need. I do the food shopping at my house. My dad drops me off, hits Target for all that kind of stuff, then picks me up. I can supply the oatmeal."

"Okay, then," Jake said. "Nothing left to do but acquire this mole here."

I made a face. I was nearest the cage. "Does it bite?"

"I wouldn't think so," Cassie said. "It usually just eats . . . I mean, I don't think it'll bite you."

I turned on her. "What does it usually eat, Cassie?"

"Well, it eats what you'd expect an underground animal to eat. It eats worms. Mostly worms."

"Oh, great," I moaned.

I stretched out my hand and Cassie opened the cage. I touched the mole and kept my hand there while I felt the mole DNA become a part of me. I suppose the mole became quiet and still, the way most animals do when you acquire them, but who could tell? It was already pretty quiet.

When it came to Tobias's turn, the mole got a bit more excited. You have to be in your own body when you acquire new DNA. And now the hawk body was Tobias's own true body. So to acquire the mole, he had to flap down to the cage and grab the poor creature with his talons.

Just as Cassie's father arrived, we left the barn and went toward the school.

The Yeerk pool is a vast, underground complex. It's like one of those covered football stadiums or whatever. In the center is the pool itself, but there is an open area all around the pool, so all together it's probably a thousand or fifteen hundred feet across. I'm guessing. We never exactly measured it.

It's big, for being a hole in the ground. It stretches beneath the school and clear over to the mall. At least the entrances do. The entrances are concealed stairways that come in from angles all around the pool. We've found entrances in the janitor's closet at school (the Yeerks eliminated that one later) and in the dressing rooms at The Gap in the mall.

<Based on the entrances we've found over time, I think the center of the Yeerk pool is right at this intersection,> Tobias said.

We were all at the intersection between the school and the mall.

"Well, we can't dig here," I said.

"We wouldn't want to," Marco pointed out. "We don't want to be right over the pool when we dig through." He made a falling motion with his hands then said, "Splash!"

"Good point," I agreed. The idea of falling into the Yeerk pool itself was nauseating.

Jake said, "However, we want to be close to the pool itself so we can tell exactly where it is when we dig through. That way we can dig a horizontal side tunnel out over the pool and use it to drop the oatmeal."

Marco nodded. "I have the strange feeling this will involve some kind of geometry I should have paid attention to in class."

"You are asking for a lot of precision, Prince Jake," Ax said. "We have no instruments. Struments. Not even primitive human instruments. Struuu-ments. Mints? In-stru-mints?"

"We have to make an educated guess, Ax. And don't call me 'prince.'"

"Yes, Prince Jake."

Tobias had come to rest on a high lamppost. Hawks have amazingly good hearing, so he could still hear us talking.

I looked up at him. "Tobias? You're the one who keeps track of entrances and stuff. What's your best estimate?"

"And don't forget, we could use some privacy for morphing," Jake said.

Tobias opened his wings and flew up and up. He inscribed a swift, irregular circle in the sky, then came back to roost. <I think I have a place.>

CHAPTER 15

It turned out to be a toolshed. It was in the backyard of a house that was empty and had a decrepit "For Sale" sign in the weeds of the overgrown front yard.

The house was on the main road, sandwiched between a convenience store and a place that sold hot tubs. There was a lot of noisy traffic going by all the time. Some distance behind the house there was a forlorn little park. Just a few trees, some picnic tables, and a lumpy sort of hill with rocks jutting out of the soil. It didn't look like anyone had lived in the house in a long time.

The toolshed was rusted tin with a dirt floor. It was empty, except for some bags of potting soil and a rake.

"Perfect," Jake declared. "A little cramped, but perfect. But once we're all in mole morph, it'll be roomy enough."

Cassie cleared her throat. "Um . . . maybe I should have mentioned this earlier. But it's not about all of us being moles at once. Not at first, anyway. I mean, only one mole can dig at a time."

We all stared at her as we let that bit of information sink in. Somehow I'd had images of us all down underground digging away together. Now I was getting a very different picture.

"We're gonna be down there alone?" Marco yelped. "Underground? Dirt pressing in all around us? No air?"

Cassie shrugged. "Well, you'll be a mole."

"Well, then it's all right," Marco said with shrill sarcasm. "We'll be moles, so it's okay to be under twenty feet of dirt with no air."

"Oh, you big baby," I said. "No problem."

I say these things. I don't know why. They just pop out of my stupid mouth.

"Ladies and gentlemen," Marco said, placing his hand on my shoulder, "we have a volunteer."

What could I say? I had to tough it through. "Okay. Fine, Weenie-boy. I'll go first."

It was hot in the little shed with all of us crammed in there. Hot and airless. And already I

83

was feeling a little claustrophobic. You know, the fear of tight spaces.

I focused my mind on the image of the mole. And by whatever weird means the morphing technology works, I began to change.

The first thing I noticed was that there was more room in the shed. The bodies that had been pressed close were getting farther away. I was shrinking.

But I wasn't shrinking at the same rate all over. My legs and arms were shrinking much, much faster.

FLUMP!

My butt hit the floor!

"Whoa!" Jake yelled. "Catch her!"

Jake and Cassie grabbed me. Just in time to keep me from falling over. Too late to save my dignity.

Marco started giggling. "Heh heh, ha ha ha ha!"

Cassie was snorting desperately, trying not to laugh.

My legs had shriveled away, leaving nothing but feet. My arms were nothing but hands. I was still a human being, but with feet alone where my legs should have been.

Jake and Cassie held my shoulders and balanced me upright. I was like one of those blow-up clowns you punch and it rolls back. I was sitting down, waving my toes and fingers and wishing I could strangle Marco.

"Wait till it's your tuuuuurn, nyarco!" I yelled. But my face chose that moment to start pushing out and out and out.

They laid me down on my face finally, since I was now about two feet long. Thick black-brown fur began to sweep across me, transforming me from mostly human to mostly mole in appearance.

My face just kept bulging outward, forming a fantastically long, ratlike snout.

But while most of me seemed to be shrinking, my hands seemed to be growing. Relative to the rest of me, anyway. I was growing hands like claw-tipped shovels. Big, flat, hairless, hard, with stubby claws on the ends of each "finger." My hands twisted as I watched, turning outward.

My eyes went dark. I thought I was totally blind. Then I realized, no, I could still see. But all I could see were vague lines between dark and light. I was practically blind, but not completely.

Almost blind. With hearing that was dim and distant, like listening through a door. Even scent was nothing special.

However, a new sense reared up to fill my brain. Touch! My nose was insanely alive and so sensitive to touch I could feel the air currents around me.

Deprived of vision and much of my hearing, I felt panic. I was supposed to go digging down in the ground like this? Blind? Half-deaf?

And yet . . . I felt the earth beneath my shovel hands and my ratlike back legs, and scraping under my belly. My nose poked at the dirt and felt its texture, moistness, hardness.

It was certainly better underground. Safer. Oh yes, far safer underground.

Besides, I was hungry.

I began to dig.

From far away I heard a voice say, "Well, she's getting right down to business, huh?"

"It still looks like a rat to me."

I dug my claws into the dirt and shoved it back with my "hands." Then again. More. And now the desire to dig was very much stronger. I had to dig! I was surrounded by big, lumbering shapes of gray on gray. When they moved I could see the shifts in the light pattern.

Dig! I could feel the warmth of the earth calling to me. In some dim part of my mind I could almost form a picture of a cozy little hole, deep down, filled with comfortable grasses and twigs and scraps of garbage.

I could curl up there when I wasn't waddling through my tunnels. The tunnels where beetles might dig through and lay their eggs for me to eat. Where, in the absolute darkness, my sensitive nose would encounter the squirming squishiness of a plump, juicy earthworm.

Oh, yes, dig!

"You know, it occurs to me, maybe she's not in total control of this morph."

"Nah. Come on. You think a mole has strong enough instincts to take over Rachel's brain?"

"Look at the way she's digging."

"Hmm. Rachel? Hey, Rachel? How you doing down there?"

Dig and dig and dig. Now my upper body was down in the warm darkness of earth. Dig harder! Get all the way under. Darkness was safety. The safety of warm, moist earth pressing in all around.

"She's not answering. She's totally gone mole on us. I wouldn't have thought moles had that powerful a set of instincts. Okay, better grab her before she gets all the way under."

Suddenly, I felt something grab me! It grabbed my tail. It was pulling me backward. I dug furiously with my shovel hands. I scrabbled at the dirt, but it was too powerful.

Up, up, up through the air! Exposed! Nothing around me but air, air, air! Emptiness!

"Hey, Rachel. It's me, Jake. Snap out of it. The mole brain has you."

I snapped out of it. It was a sensation like . . . well, like emerging from a tunnel into daylight. I was back! I was me. Me, staring through those utterly useless mole eyes.

<Did not!> I said.

"Yeah, right," I heard Marco say.

<I was just trying to get on with it. Hey, I'm here to dig, right? So I was digging, jerk.>

Jake put me back down by the shallow hole I'd made.

"Ooookay, Rachel. You were not having trouble. Everything was fine."

I went back to work. But now the earth didn't seem so inviting or warm.

CHAPTER 16

Down and down I dug.

Till my entire body was in the dirt. And now I was no longer hiding beneath the mole's mind. I was a human being, digging blindly into the dirt.

Why should it have been terrifying? Why?

Was it the way the dirt pressed in all around me? The fact that I could not possibly turn around? I couldn't breathe! Only I *could* breathe. Yes, I was breathing. But that panic, that terror of suffocating in a dark place, kept rearing up. I could push it down, I could reason with myself, but that fear of suffocation was too strong.

I was buried alive.

Correction: I was burying *myself* alive.

Down I went, down and down. I knew I should

be digging a vertical hole, but it was impossible. The mole couldn't dig that way. The best it could do was slope downward.

I dug. How long, I don't know. It seemed like a very long time.

And then, quite suddenly, I couldn't stand it anymore. I needed air! I tried to back up, but no! I couldn't move that way.

<Come on, Rachel. Get a grip, kid. Get a grip!> I said to myself. <Just dig a turnaround. That's it. A little more off the sides. Yeah. Hang in there.>

No air! Oh, lord, I'm buried alive!

<No! No! Hold on. Keep digging out a turn-around.>

I scraped madly with my "hands," shoving the dirt back beneath my body to be shoved back by my hind legs.

And slowly a chamber began to appear. A hole a few inches wide on either side of me. I tried turning. Not yet. Dig some more. Dig in blind darkness.

Finally . . . yes! I could turn around. My sensitive nose felt the empty, open tunnel ahead of me. It was crumbly and far from perfect, but it was a tunnel.

I raced down it, squeezing through the tight spaces, desperate, desperate for air!

My nose emerged into light. It seemed blinding now.

"She's back," Cassie said. "Rachel, are you okay?"

<Yeah. Yeah. Fine,> I lied.

"How far did you get? You were down there for twenty minutes."

Twenty minutes? No. It had been an hour at least.

<I . . . um, I don't know.> I tried to visualize the tunnel I'd never actually seen but only felt. How long was it? <I guess it was, I don't know, probably only three feet.>

"Three feet straight down?" Jake said with a whistle. "That's pretty good. The top of the Yeerk pool dome is probably what, fifty feet down maybe?"

<Not straight down,> I said. <The mole can't dig straight down. It's just barely downhill. Maybe a foot deep.>

<Oh, man,> Tobias groaned. <This is going to take us forever.>

We took one-hour shifts. Between shifts those of us who weren't digging or standing guard walked down to the Mickey D's and bought fries and Cokes.

Six hours of digging till we had each done our shift. The day was over. We couldn't stay any longer. We had to head home.

"Someone should carry a string down in to see how far we got," Marco suggested.

No one volunteered. No one even moved. We were a haggard, unhappy-looking bunch of kids. Sweating and pale from the stress of fear and the constant morphing.

"I'll do it," I said. "It's my turn."

I morphed and Cassie tied the end of a string around my tail.

Down into the tunnels again. We'd each gone as far as we could, then dug a turnaround. Six turnarounds. I counted them as I passed each one by.

I would have been sweating if I were human. It was hot and close. Very close. Like being in a coffin. That image kept coming up. Like being in a coffin. Like being buried alive. Like you wanted to kick and scream to get out, only no one would hear you because you were underground. Buried alive.

Then my nose touched a wall. The end. I had reached the end of the tunnel. You'd think I'd have been relieved. But now the pressure to get out out OUT drove me to the edge of panic.

I could barely control myself. Barely keep from screaming.

I raced back along that tunnel as if something were chasing me. Was that light up ahead? No, I'd only passed three turnarounds. Or was it four?

Finally, I poked my snout up out of the

ground, crawled free of the hole, and began to demorph instantly.

Ax was in his own body, having been in human morph too long. He measured out the string I'd carried down the hole. <Would you like the measurement in feet or in meters?>

I was human enough to be able to see Marco roll his eyes. "Whatever."

<The total length of the tunnel is approximately forty-one feet long. I believe the slope ratio is about six to one. One foot down for every six feet of tunnel. That would mean we·tunneled down approximately six point eight feet.>

I was emerging into my human body now and still trying to shake off the unholy willies. "Six lousy feet!"

<Closer to seven lousy feet,> Ax corrected.

<Oh, man,> Tobias moaned. <If we're right and we have to dig down fifty feet, that would take us a week. You've got to be kidding! I'm a bird. I have no business being in a tunnel.>

I almost agreed. In fact, I almost said, "Forget it! I'm outta here."

But I didn't. In fact, I was the strongest voice for going forward. See, I wasn't going to let the claustrophobia scare me. I wasn't going to let fear dictate what I did.

Or maybe I was just a fool.

CHAPTER 17

We got better at digging as we became more experienced. But then we found ourselves running into rocky levels no mole was designed to dig through. We had to figure out ways around the rocks. Long, time-consuming ways around boulders.

And we could only dig after school. We'd bring our homework and sit in that stifling shed and quiz each other on history or science. Ax would stand there, listening gravely to the history, and laughing at the primitive nature of our science.

One by one we'd go down that hole. We timed it out so the next person was always in morph and ready to go. Four more days we dug. Till

Cassie came back up and said, <I think we're blocked. It's solid rock.>

"We are not blocked," I said. "We have not been doing all this just to end up blocked. There has to be a way."

So down I went. Like an idiot. Like I was all excited about digging the stupid tunnel.

Ax had calculated we were twenty-five feet down. Down through loose topsoil and clay and gravel. Down and down I scurried, pushing ahead with my little back feet, always clearing the tunnel of fallen dirt with my spade feet.

I reached the end. The darkness was so absolute that no eye could see. Let alone a mole's eye.

My nose touched the end of the tunnel. I began to dig. Rock. I moved left. Rock. I started thinking, hoping almost, that Cassie had been right. No more digging. No more tunnel. No more being buried alive.

But then I found it. The seam between rocks. My nose felt it. I dug away some dirt and the seam grew. Yes, there was an opening.

I hesitated. Did I really have to tell the others? They would take my word for it if I said Cassie was right. No one else was going to come down here to check. No one liked this any more than I did.

I dug some more. And then . . .

<What?>

Air! A breeze.

<No way.>

But it *was* a breeze. Faint, and smelling heavy and damp and nasty. But a definite breeze. Air was flowing up between the rocks.

<Hey, guys?> I called up in thought-speak. But they were out of range. No answer came.

I dug away more dirt and now the breeze was stronger still. There was enough space for me to push my body through. But I sensed emptiness beyond.

I turned around and raced back to the surface.

<I think I hit a cave or something,> I said. <Cassie was right, it's rocky. But there's a breeze coming up between the rocks.>

Jake checked his watch. "Too late for today. We'll hit it tomorrow. It's Saturday. We'll have more time."

So on Saturday we were back. Rested and refreshed. Or as rested and refreshed as you can be after a night of nightmares where you're trapped in a coffin screaming, "Let me out, I'm not dead!"

This time we all went down together. We dug out a larger area around the fissure in the rock. We made it large enough for all of us to fit. And somehow, as creepy as it still was, it was more or less comforting to know that everyone was down there with me.

Until it occurred to me that now there was no one on the surface to rescue us. The tunnel could collapse, we could be trapped . . . what could I do, morph to human? Under twenty-five feet of dirt?

Everyone took turns digging away the last of the dirt. Our noses told us we were standing around a crack that went down and down into the rock.

<This just gets to be more and more fun, doesn't it?> Marco said sarcastically. <Now it's solid rock.>

<Better than digging through dirt,> I said.

<Oh, yeah? Guess again. We're moles. If a dirt tunnel collapses on us we can dig our way out. What do we do if rocks collapse in on us?>

He was right. I had to force myself to stay very still and not start running. If I started running, I'd never stop.

<If you're scared, I'll go in,> I said.

<I'm scared,> Marco confirmed. <Help yourself.>

There must be something kind of liberating, just being able to say "I'm scared" like it's no big deal. I can't do that. I don't know why. I just can't.

I pushed my sleek mole body down into the

rock. It was rough, unworn rock. Rock that had been split open by pressure. I shoved forward. The path twisted and turned, but not too much.

If I demorphed in here, my human body would be a hundred times too big. What would happen? Would I become a part of the rock? Would I be able to scream and scream with no one hearing me, no one able to help?

<Get a grip!> I ordered myself. <Stop torturing yourself. It's going to be okay.>

Suddenly . . .

<Aaaahhhh!>

I was falling! Falling blind.

CHAPTER 18

Falling!

<Aaaahhhh!>

<Rachel!>

WHUMPF!

<Rachel! What's the matter?> Cassie's thought-speak voice.

I landed on my back. I landed on something almost soft. Something that reeked in my mole nose.

I was still in total, absolute darkness. I couldn't see anything. But I knew I was in a vast, open space. The Yeerk pool? No, of course not. There would be light there.

But definitely an open space. Large. Quite large.

And then I realized I was not alone.

I didn't know what they were, but I felt their presence above me. Many, many of them.

<Rachel!> It was Jake now. <Answer if you can.>

<I'm okay,> I said. <I . . . I guess I fell into some kind of a cave.>

<Do you see a guy in a cape and a really cool car?> Marco asked.

<What?> I was too preoccupied to care about his dumb jokes.

<The Batcave,> he said. <I'm thinking you fell into the Batcave.>

It wasn't until that moment that I realized whose presence I felt above me.

<Actually, Marco, I think maybe it *is* a bat cave. Come on down. You can jump. It's a nice, soft landing on a bat-poop mattress.>

One by one they came, dropping down beside me. And soon we were six blind moles wallowing in mostly dried bat guano.

Now that I was out of the tunnel, out of the confined space, I wanted to laugh. <Well, this is pretty glorious, huh? We have tunneled our way into a major bat-poop deposit. A whole week, and we have reached a bat cave. You know what I think? I think this whole thing has been cursed. And I think it's all my fault. I should have let that Edelman guy just splat on the concrete.>

<We can't back out now,> Marco said. <I have thirty-six boxes of maple-and-ginger instant oatmeal at home. In easy-open single serving pouches.>

<We should demorph,> Cassie said.

<Why?> Tobias asked. <So we can really enjoy the lovely ambience?>

<I was thinking since we're in a bat cave, maybe we should go into our own bat morphs,> Cassie said.

<Oh. I don't have a bat morph,> Tobias said.

<Easily fixed in here,> Cassie said with a laugh. <I'll bet there are a few hundred thousand bats hanging from the roof of this cave. Just hanging around and waiting for someone to come along and acquire their DNA.>

<You're awfully cheerful,> Jake grumbled. <We're in a cave way underground with no way out except a mole tunnel we can't reach anymore.>

<No, no, no,> Cassie said. <Wrong. Don't you realize? The bats fly out of here at dusk. Out. As in *out*? As in *exit*?>

<Hey! She's right!> I yelled. <We won't be buried alive in here. Not that I was worried or anything.>

<No, we'll just be buried in bat poop,> Marco muttered. <Let's morph to bat like Cassie said.>

Yes, bat was a good idea. If you're going to be

in a bat cave, best to be a bat. But first we had to pass through our own natural bodies.

And oh, was that not fun.

You think it's grim being a mole in a bat cave? Try being a human. For one thing, the cave was less high than we'd thought. For another thing, we all passed through the same helpless stage where we had big, swollen human bodies with tiny little feet and arms.

"Ah, MAN!" Marco moaned. "Buried in bat —"

"Guano," Cassie said, supplying the word.

"Yeah, guano. That's what I was gonna say. Guano."

"This is so guh-ROSS!" I yelled.

My arms and legs reappeared and I had to stick my palms down in the stuff to raise up. The only good thing was that the awfulness of the grossness completely distracted me from the claustrophobia.

<What are you whining about, Rachel?> Tobias snapped grumpily. <Try having feathers in this stuff.>

I raised myself up. I stood up. I raised my head. And that's when I made the discovery about the cave not being as high as we'd thought.

You see, my head was entirely surrounded by soft, warm, fuzzy bats.

There was really only one thing to do.

"Marco," I said. "Be sure and stretch out. Up on your tiptoes now."

"Aaaahhhh!" he yelped. "Oh, really funny, Rachel. That was so mature!"

"What, I should suffer and you shouldn't, just because you're short?"

And then, weird as it seems, we all burst out giggling. Thirty feet underground in a bat cave so dark you might as well be blind, lost, scared, and smeared with bat guano, we got the giggles.

CHAPTER 19

"Here. Have a bat," I said. I held one for Tobias. I wasn't afraid of bats. I'd been one.

<Thanks.>

"Watch out, he'll eat it," Marco said.

"You know," Jake said in a conversational tone as we waited for Tobias to acquire the bat, "from the point where Edelman said 'maple and ginger oatmeal,' I should have known this was going to end stupidly."

"*Instant* maple and ginger oatmeal," Cassie said.

"Battles that involve oatmeal are just never going to end up being historic, you know?" Jake went on. "Gettysburg? No major oatmeal involvement. The Battle of Midway? Neither side used oatmeal. Desert Storm? No oatmeal."

<Excuse me, but what *is* oatmeal?> Ax asked.

"It's a kind of food," Cassie explained.

<Is it tasty?>

"You can think about food here? Here?" Marco said. "In bat-poop land?"

"Battle of Bunker Hill? No oatmeal used by the British, no oatmeal used by the Americans," Jake went on. "D-Day? No mention of oatmeal."

<Okay, I'm ready,> Tobias said.

"Let's do it, and then let's get out of this place," I said.

I focused my mind on the bat. The bat DNA had come from a common brown bat. Not a very big animal. More like a mouse with wings.

It was a strange sensation. I was shrinking. Probably. But I couldn't see anything. So I couldn't see myself getting smaller. Couldn't see any of the changes.

In the absolute darkness I was left with just my sense of hearing. I heard things I seldom noticed. I heard my thick, human bones grinding and suddenly squishing as they went liquid. I heard a sound like my stomach rumbling from hunger. Only it was the sound of my stomach and all my internal organs shifting and moving. Some organs shrank. Some basically disappeared. All of it was happening inside me at a point when I didn't even know if I was five feet tall or five inches.

I reached with my hands to touch my face and "see" how much I'd morphed. But my hands were restricted. They were weirdly jointed. And when I moved them I heard a faint sound like leather being folded.

I flapped my arms. Yes, I had wings. The paper-thin leather of bat wings.

And then, I felt that most vital of bat powers: I felt the echolocation. I fired an ultrasonic blast. Sound waves pitched higher than any human ear would ever hear. But I heard them. They came bouncing back to me and I heard every distorted, twisted, shattered echo.

<Oh!> I said in amazement. I'd been a bat only once before, and only for a short time. I'd forgotten the stunning array of information that comes from echolocating.

It was as if I'd been blind and allowed to see.

Not "see" the way humans see. But to see shapes, edges, openness, and narrowness. I fired another burst and I "saw" the edges of a thousand bats clustered above us. I saw their tiny, doglike faces and their big feathery ears as they hung down with wings folded demurely.

It was as if all the world were drawn with pen and ink. Edges and outlines, no hint of color. And each picture was only a flash, only there as long as the echoes lasted.

Now the others all began echolocating, and I redoubled my own efforts.

Yes! I could see the cave. A comic book drawing of a cave, thin lines and thick ones.

I flapped my wings and lifted off heavily, rising from the floor of the cave. I took a quick turn around, absolutely confident of where I was flying.

<It's not quite like seeing, but it beats being blind,> Cassie said, sighing with relief.

I realized the others had been as stressed as I was by the utter darkness.

<To the Batmobile, Robin,> Marco said.

<How about if we just get out of this place?> Tobias suggested.

<I'm with that,> Jake said.

We flew. Through the cave, which wound and twisted, always beneath hanging bat stalactites, and above a carpet of bat-guano stalagmites.

I could feel the way out. I could feel the slight changes of air pressure, the changes of temperature that showed the way out. But then . . .

<You guys feel that?> I asked.

<It's coming from our left,> Ax said. <My echolocation is showing an opening. But not an opening to the outside.>

<Oh, man,> I moaned. I could feel the near-

ness of the cave opening. But I could also feel this other exit. I had a pretty good sense of where that second exit might lead.

<We *could* just go home,> Jake said. He was offering us all a way out. Go home, forget about it for now. He didn't want to "order" us to go on if we weren't up for it.

Everyone in a group has a role to play. At least that's how it always works out. My role was to say, "Let's do it. Let's go. That's what we came here for."

But I was tired. And I'd had a really, really bad few days digging down to this stupid cave.

So I said, <Let's do it. That's what we came here for.>

Sometimes it's hard to get out of a role once you've started playing the part.

CHAPTER 20

It was a vertical crack in solid rock. In places it was no more than eight inches wide. At its best it was a foot wide.

With wing tips scraping the rock wall, we flew. Through a world seen only in echolocating sketches, we flew.

<Cool! This is so *Star Wars*!> I said, genuinely enjoying it. <Remember when they're attacking the Death Star and —>

Suddenly, the crack plunged downward. Down ten feet and then —

<Whoa ho!>

We blew out into a world of light! I could see again. People think bats are blind, but they're not. I could see a vast, open area lit with stadium lights down below us.

We fluttered in a circle at the top of a dome. The crack we'd entered through was high up, almost at the very peak of the dome. And down below us was the Yeerk pool.

<Well,> Jake said, <we found our way into the Yeerk pool.>

<Yeah. Great,> Cassie said darkly. <Now what?>

<Now we figure out how to get that oatmeal in here and feed it to a bunch of human-Controllers,> Tobias said.

<You know . . . maybe we don't have to give it to human-Controllers,> Cassie said. <I don't know why it didn't occur to me before. But it's the Yeerk that can't resist the stuff, right? So why don't we dump it right in the Yeerk pool itself?>

<Would it work?> Tobias wondered. <I thought all Yeerks ate was Kandrona rays. Do they even have mouths?>

<Yes,> Ax said. <Yeerks have mouths. Or what humans would think of as mouths. Actually, if I remember my exo-biology classes, and sadly, I sometimes —>

<Fell asleep,> I said. <Yeah, we know. You didn't like exo-biology class.>

<I didn't fall asleep,> Ax said, sounding injured. <I merely let my mind wander, and be-

came very calm and restful and not completely alert.>

<Did you snore when you got all calm and restful and not completely alert?>

<The point is, on occasion I *would* pay *some* attention in class. And I believe that Yeerks have something called osmosis nodes. It's what they use to absorb Kandrona rays, but they absorb other nutrients as well. They absorb from the liquid of the Yeerk pool.>

<So if we dump enough instant maple and ginger oatmeal in this Yeerk pool, they should absorb it, right?> Jake asked.

<Yes, Prince Jake. At least, I think so. Maybe.>

<Oh, good, I just love risking my life for a "maybe,"> Marco said.

<Hey,> Tobias said. <I think we have company. Over there.>

I looked around. I saw two shiny steel balls. Each was about the size of a beach ball. My echolocation confirmed their size. And they were moving toward us through the air.

<Hunter robots!> Ax yelled. <We should leave!>

<Why?> I asked.

But at that very moment, I had my answer.

TSEEEEEWWW! TSEEEEEWWW! TSEEEEEWWW!

Three narrow Dracon beams fired from the

balls. I felt a sharp pain in my right wing. I smelled something burning. And when I looked, I saw a neat, round hole the size of a quarter burned through the leather of my wing.

<Okay, let's leave,> I said. I turned and headed for the crack, with all the others alongside me.

TSEEEEEWWW! TSEEEEEWWW! TSEEEEEWWW!

<Aaarrgghh!>

Tobias! He was hit. He was falling, tumbling downward, down to the Yeerk pool below us. I had a weird flash of poor Mr. Edelman falling, and then down I went after Tobias.

Bats aren't all that fast in flight. Fortunately, Tobias had a lot of experience flying. He managed to use his one good wing to slow his fall. I caught him and grabbed with my tiny but strong little bat feet. Ax and Jake were there in a flash and we flapped madly, hauling him upward.

But the hunter robots were closing in on us.

TSEEEEEWWW! TSEEEEEWWW! TSEEEEEWWW!

<Aaahhh! I've been hit!> Ax yelled. His flying weakened. It was no longer even possible to get Tobias back up to the crack.

<We're bats,> Tobias gasped. <I can hang.>

I realized what he was telling me. If we could get him to the rocks, any rocks, he could latch on and hang. Not exactly a solution, but the only thing we could do.

Down swooped Jake, just in time. He slammed into us deliberately, pushing us toward the sloping rock ceiling. Tobias scrabbled madly and managed to grab some rock with his feet.

The hunter robots came on, almost leisurely. Maybe they had enough intelligence to realize that they had us cold.

<Ax! Do those things have any weak points?> Marco yelled.

Cassie and Marco had flown off through all this. I couldn't blame them. But I had wondered . . .

<Visual aiming system,> Ax groaned. <A lens. Like a human camera lens.>

<I see it,> Cassie yelled.

BONK!

BONK!

My echolocation "saw" the tiny rocks go flying. They were like bombs dropped from dive-bombers. Cassie and Marco had each grabbed small rocks, dived toward the robots, and released them.

One must have hit. One of the robots began to veer away like it was lost.

But the other was just twenty feet away when it fired. I swept my good wing over Tobias, trying to shield him.

TSEEEEEWWW! TSEEEEEWWW!

The Dracon beam burned the wing off. Clear off. I had a stump of a bat arm. And I fell like a stone.

Down, down, down through the damp air.

Down to the Yeerk pool.

CHAPTER 21

I fell.

I saw Jake and Cassie come for me. But I knew. I knew they couldn't make it.

<Back off, you idiots!> I screamed. And then I hit.

SPUH-LOOSH!

I landed on my back. It knocked the wind out of me. I gasped for air. But I was under the surface.

I was in liquid the color of lead. But living, seething water. The Yeerks were everywhere! All around me.

I bobbed to the surface. I tried to fire my echolocation, but the liquid kept rolling over me in sluggish little swells.

I was in the Yeerk pool!

That awful fact was like an explosion in my brain. They were everywhere! All around me! They would get me now. I couldn't escape. I flapped my single sodden wing, but all I managed to do was churn the water a little.

I started to call out to my friends. But no. No. They would kill themselves trying to rescue me. No.

Only . . . what if the Yeerks made me a Controller? I would betray all my friends. I wouldn't be able not to.

They can only make you a Controller if you demorph, I told myself. *They can't do anything to a bat. Too small a brain for a Yeerk slug. Stay in morph.*

But then I began to notice something. The Yeerks didn't seem to be paying any attention to me. It was like they didn't even notice the presence of a floundering bat.

Maybe they didn't.

Those hunter robots weren't there specifically to kill us. They must have been programmed to attack any animal. The Yeerks were being careful. They knew we'd infiltrated the Yeerk pool before. So they had brought the Bio-scans to the entrances. And they had activated the hunter robots. But a lot of innocent animals must have been fried over time. Other bats had probably wandered in.

So I was probably not the first animal to end up in the Yeerk pool with a Dracon beam wound.

THUD.

A Yeerk bumped into me.

I froze. Nothing.

SLOOOP.

A Yeerk brushed against me. Nothing.

It hit me then. <Oh, man. They're blind. They can't see when they're in the pool. They can't see without using some host's eyes.>

So how did they find their way back to their host when it was time? Smell? Sound? Some other sense?

I looked up and saw the domed rock roof so high up above. I looked for my friends, but I couldn't see them. Maybe they were safe. Maybe not.

If they had been taken prisoner I had to save them. But I couldn't thought-speak. They'd probably assume I'd been badly injured. Or worse. If I called them, they might be destroyed trying to save me.

What should I do?

If the Yeerks couldn't see a bat, could they see a human? I could morph to shark and go rampaging through the pool, eating the vile slugs till one of the Controllers on shore saw my dorsal fin and burned me.

There was a vaguely circular current in the pool.

I was drifting around in a lazy semicircle. Coming closer and closer to that evil steel pier where they dragged the hosts and thrust their heads under the water to allow the Yeerks to re-enter.

Under the pier! If I was going to demorph, that was the place.

Closer, closer I drifted. Closer, and I could hear the shouts. The cries. The screams. The utter despair.

"No! No! Let me go, you have no right! Let me go, I have children who —"

The voice was cut off. The woman's head had been shoved brutally down under the surface. And seconds later, she stood up, perfectly calm. A Controller once more.

I could see the pier clearly, although from a very low angle. Bored Hork-Bajir-Controllers dragged unwilling humans and unwilling Hork-Bajir to the end of the pier, kicked their legs out from under them, and thrust their heads into the pool.

It was just a day's work for the Hork-Bajir. The threats and pleading meant nothing. They'd heard it all before. Hundreds of times. Thousands and thousands of times.

The idea of morphing to a shark and laying waste through the Yeerk pool was starting to seem better and better. How I hated the foul slugs that surged and frolicked around me.

But that would be a suicide mission. Maybe there was still some way to stay alive.

The pier was coming closer. It was very low, just inches above the water surface.

What should I do?

Well, Rachel, I thought, *you sure don't want to end your life as a one-winged bat.*

I began to demorph.

There, floating amidst the enemy, I began to emerge back into human form.

I was under the pier!

I reached, hoping I had something like a hand. Rough, stubby fingers scraped along the steel underside of the pier.

I thrust a face that was half-human and half-bat up into the three inches of air space.

I could see up through the gaps in the steel planks. I saw Hork-Bajir feet and the short Hork-Bajir tail go by overhead.

I saw human feet being dragged.

"Please, no. Please, no. Please, no," the man whimpered.

I was larger now, a lot larger, so more and more Yeerk slugs were banging into me or brushing past me.

Oh, for my hammerhead shark's razor teeth.

But that wasn't the way to survive.

CHAPTER 22

Fully human, I began to morph again.

I needed to be right at the end of the pier for it to work. I was going to get very, very small. The distances had to be small, too.

I was going to do the one morph I'd sworn never to do again.

I shrank. As I shrank I pulled myself closer to the end of the pier. When my arms became useless, I paddled.

I shrank and shrank till the low roof of the pier over my head seemed miles away.

An extra set of legs extruded from my midriff.

Antennae shot from my forehead.

My body was severely squeezed into three segments. I was an hourglass with a head.

My skin grew hard as fingernails. Just like a cockroach's exoskeleton. But I was not morphing a roach. I was going much, much smaller. A cockroach would be visible. A cockroach would be an elephant compared to the animal I was becoming.

I was less than an inch long and still shrinking. Becoming the most terrifying animal I had ever become.

I was becoming an ant.

I fought my way continually to the surface. I couldn't afford to be trapped under the water. And soon, my natural buoyancy and small size kept me riding easily atop the swells.

I took a last look around with my fading eyes. I knew what was coming. I knew I'd be almost blind. I needed to pick a direction and know where I was.

A huge pillar, fifty times as big as a redwood, loomed up in front of me. Right in front of me.

My eyes went off like someone had thrown a switch. I was nearly blind. More blind than a mole. All I could see were vague, distorted lines between dark and light. Shadows. But I knew where I was.

My six ant legs splayed out. They pressed down on a rubbery surface — the water. It was like trying to walk on a trampoline. And my legs kept poking through the surface.

But mostly I could do it. I could walk on the water. Or at least stand. Forward movement was very difficult.

Fortunately, the water did that for me. A swell came along. I felt it well up beneath me, a vast, powerful wave that set me rocketing up and up on its crest.

I was surfing the Yeerk pool.

SPLUSH!

The wave crashed against the pylon. A steel wall loomed up before me, nothing but darkness to my ant eyes. I grabbed. I set my tiny claws grabbing wildly, grabbing at anything solid.

And then the water fell away beneath me. I had grabbed the steel pylon! Tiny surface irregularities, the very grain of the metal itself, were all I needed.

Up I raced. Up to escape the next swell.

It splashed. I felt the vibrations as the water hit the pylon. Felt the air move as it was displaced by the tiny, but huge-to-me, upward surge.

The top of the water swept my back feet, but I had four more legs firmly attached, and I powered them with all my human will.

I felt the ant's mindless, machine instincts. They wouldn't be any trouble. I had morphed the ant before. I was prepared. Besides, the ant was far from anything familiar. Far from the world of smell it inhabited.

Up I went, climbing and climbing. Always upward.

Ahead of me I sensed warmth. Body warmth and the smells of a living thing. Some poor creature, human or Hork-Bajir, or some foul, vile Taxxon, was being reinfested.

I raced forward, hanging upside down as I ran. Grabbing the encrustations and irregularities of the underside of the pier.

Upside down, inches from the water, I ran and ran and didn't even slow down when I found myself no longer on steel but on fabric.

Then, up and up! I felt myself flying upward at an insane speed. But still I clung to the ropes that were threads in a cotton shirt.

The host had been reinfested. I was on a Controller. I was on his shirt, scuttling for cover beneath a damp collar.

<Hah! Let's see the hunter robots find me here,> I said triumphantly.

CHAPTER 23

I was alive. I had escaped from the Yeerk pool itself!

But I couldn't be elated. I didn't know what had happened to my friends. For all I knew, they had not made it.

I was riding safe and secure, clutching to twisted cotton threads the size of bridge cables.

<Cheap shirt,> I muttered to no one. I could feel the roughness of the fabric.

Eventually, I was going to have to jump. Hopefully, the person I was on would go into one of the buildings. Hopefully, he was not going to head straight back out of the Yeerk pool to the outside world.

I didn't want to leave the place. Not yet. I had to find out what had happened to the others.

I felt a breeze blowing across me. I felt the fabric ripple. We were walking. How fast, how far? No way to know.

Had the quality of the light changed? Impossible to say. I had to take a shot in the dark. Had to guess.

I raced out from under the collar and headed uphill. I climbed up onto what I assumed was a shoulder.

Could I do this? Could ants jump? Only one way to find out. I ran out to the end of the shoulder. I carefully released the grip of each of my six legs. One by one. Then I crouched and pushed off.

I guess the movement of the person who'd been carrying me was enough to make it work. I didn't so much jump as I rolled off the edge.

I fell! Forever. I swear it took me ten seconds to hit the ground, and in that time I tumbled, totally out of control, mostly blind. I had no way of knowing when I would hit. And even though I knew an animal as small as an ant wouldn't be hurt by the fall, it was frightening.

POOMPF!

I hit. I rolled onto my legs. Where was I? I felt around with my antennae. A smooth surface.

Okay. Fine. I was on a floor. Where I could easily be stepped on. Great. Now to find someplace dark where I could demorph without being seen.

I raced across the floor, totally unaware of where I might be. Then, darkness. But what did it mean? Was it a different room? Or had I just crawled under a cupboard or something?

I ran on for a while, making sure that the space I was in was large enough. Then I began to demorph.

It's a long, long way up from the ground going from ant to human. But my eyes didn't return till I was halfway demorphed. I looked around. Dark, but not the dark of the cave. There was dim, gray light here. It outlined sharp edges and right angles.

A storeroom. There were boxes piled all around me. They seemed to be made of blue plastic. I leaned against one as I finished returning to my own body.

Human again! I looked around. My eyes had had plenty of time to adjust to the gloom. There was writing on some of the boxes. But not any alphabet I'd ever seen.

There was a square pad outlined in red, just an inch on each side. "Well, why not?" I muttered. I pressed the pad. Instantly the top of the box came loose with a sound like a vacuum seal

126

breaking. It sounded like when someone opens a can of coffee.

I looked inside. Then I smiled. I reached in and lifted out a hand-size Dracon beam.

"Cool."

The grip was weird. Designed for Hork-Bajir hands. But that was okay. Right by my thumb there was a slide. It went up and down. "Power settings," I decided. I had to use my middle finger to reach the trigger.

Sudden light!

A door opened. A Hork-Bajir warrior was framed there. He blinked once in the darkness.

I raised my hand and squeezed the trigger.

TSEEEWWW!

The Hork-Bajir dropped like a sack of dirty laundry.

I stepped over to him. He was still breathing. I was breathing, too, in ragged gasps.

"So, that was the low-power setting," I said. Then, "What's keeping you?"

A human voice! Female. I ducked back into the darkness.

She stopped when she saw the Hork-Bajir stretched out on the floor. She was just about to yell when . . .

TSEEEWWWW!

Down she went, sprawling right across the Hork-Bajir. She groaned once, then passed out.

I looked at the Dracon beam in my hand. "Cool. Phasers on stun, Captain."

I took the woman's shoes. As always, you can't morph shoes or bulky clothing. I took her blazer, too. It wasn't a bad blazer. I checked the label. "DKNY. Excellent. A little big for me, but okay."

I pulled my hair back into a ponytail. The blazer was large, the shoes were half a size too small, and the glasses I took from her face made the world seem a little distorted around the edges. But all in all, it wasn't a bad look. And I wanted to look good for my first trip around the Yeerk pool as a human.

I stepped out of the storeroom into the office outside. No one there. A second office outside that one. A man sat there. He was wearing a cotton shirt with a collar. He'd been my ride. Before he could turn around, I fired.

TSEEEEWWWW!

He crumpled in his chair and looked like he was asleep. Which, of course, he was.

I slid the Dracon beam into the pocket of the blazer. And then I stepped out into the world of the Yeerk pool.

CHAPTER 24

I was slightly tense.

I was walking around the Yeerk pool complex, wearing someone else's coat and shoes and glasses. I was carrying a Dracon beam. The smart thing to do would be to head for the nearest exit.

But I had to see if the others were okay. Which meant searching the entire complex.

The Yeerk pool itself is a sort of pond. But all around it is a base, with warehouses, armories, administration buildings, a motor pool, and a cafeteria for each of the major species of Controllers.

It was always being enlarged. Around the edges were human construction equipment:

Caterpillar earthmovers and backhoes and dump trucks.

But the evil heart of the complex was the Yeerk pool itself, and the cages where hosts — human and Hork-Bajir — were kept. Some of them shouted threats and obscenities. Others just sat wearily on the ground. They were the creatures whose Yeerks were in the pool at the moment.

There was a nicer area, almost like a beach club, where "voluntary" hosts hung out. Some humans. A lot of Taxxons. Both areas were larger and busier than when I'd last been there. There had to be fifty or even a hundred hosts in those cages.

Wait a minute, I thought. *There are a lot more than a hundred Yeerks in the pool.*

Of course. Obviously, a lot of them were Yeerks awaiting fresh hosts.

I considered. What would happen if I aimed the Dracon beam right at the pool and fired at maximum power?

You'd never get the others back, that's what would happen.

A pair of Hork-Bajir marched by me. I stiffened, but they had no interest in me. I was just another human-Controller as far as they were concerned.

Then another pair of Hork-Bajir came by at a

run. I followed them with my eyes. There were other Hork-Bajir, all rushing toward the edge of the Yeerk pool nearest the steel pier where they unloaded the Yeerks.

I drifted after them. I had to look cool, calm. No matter what. I couldn't look out of place.

But what I saw, there in the center of a circle of Hork-Bajir, made me want to cry out.

Ax!

He was demorphed. Fully Andalite. And there were no less than thirty Hork-Bajir warriors around him, all with Dracon beams leveled.

An Andalite can almost always beat one Hork-Bajir. Usually two. But not thirty. Ax was trapped.

He seemed calm. Or maybe just resigned.

I looked around for the others. I didn't see them. I reminded myself they could be in any number of bodies. Probably they were okay. Probably.

I hoped he would notice me. It might encourage him. But Ax was facing a sea of angry, triumphant faces. He had a lot to look at.

Two big Hork-Bajir stepped forward and very carefully slapped a metallic rope around his legs and arms. Then, even more carefully, they slid a sort of sheath over Ax's deadly tail blade.

Once Ax was helpless, they shoved him rudely onto his side and dragged him off through the dirt.

"An Andalite! Here!" someone said.

I glanced toward the voice. A distinguished-looking older woman.

"Yeah," I said. "I wonder if he was alone."

She snorted. "Andalite scum. Always skulking about, passing as some sort of animal or bug with their morphing technology. They caught two others. Or at least they think they did. A pair of bats." She grinned. "They could just be bats, I suppose. But we'll find out soon. The Visser is coming." She laughed an evil, somewhat frightened laugh. "He'll find them out."

I tried to mimic her laugh. "Oh yes, the Visser will take care of the Andalite scum."

"I wish I could stay and watch," she said. "But I have to get back. My host is a judge and there's an important case I must prepare for."

She walked away. I made a mental note of her face and occupation. I also made a note of the fact that she was lying. She didn't want to be anywhere near Visser Three. Which just proved she was smart. The Visser had a temper. And when the Visser got mad, heads always rolled. Literally.

So. Two bats and Ax. That left two of us not accounted for. Where would they be keeping the bats?

Duh, Rachel The same place they were dragging Ax.

I began to follow the drag marks. They led toward a low windowless building. There was a sign above the door. It was in lettering I didn't recognize. But there was a feeling about the place. A bad feeling.

Should I rush in and try to save Ax and the other two? No, there was no rush yet. Nothing would happen till Visser Three arrived.

<Okay. How about Rachel? Rachel? Are you listening?>

It was Marco! I glanced around. But of course I couldn't see anything. Marco could be in any kind of morph.

<Rachel, it's me, Marco. If you can hear me, Jake, Tobias, and Ax have all been taken. I'm trying to contact you and Cassie. Are you there? Can you answer?>

I could have cried from frustration. In my own human body, I couldn't use thought-speak. It was a relief to know Marco was still free.

<No? Well, I hope you're okay. I'll try again later.>

I had reached the door of the sinister building. Now what?

Suddenly, a commotion. A small knot of humans and one Hork-Bajir were coming toward me. Or at least toward the door.

"I don't know how it got there!" a human voice wailed. "I'm telling you it's a mistake!" She was young. No more than eighteen. She was scared but helpless in the grip of the Hork-Bajir.

An older, male human-Controller shook his head. "You can tell it to the Visser. He'll be here soon."

"No!" the young woman gasped. "It's a huge mistake!"

"It's a mistake, all right," the man said. He reached into the backpack the girl was carrying. He lifted out a small Rubbermaid container. He shoved it in the girl's face. "What do you call this?"

"It's . . . it's just cereal. It's something the humans call raisin bran. Human bodies need fiber in order to function properly, so —"

The man cut her off. He opened the Rubbermaid and sniffed it. He held it out for her to see. "No raisins. Don't lecture me about humans. I've been in this host body for two years. And I know the smell of maple and ginger. Fool. You're as stupid as the humans with their drugs. Never thought I'd see self-respecting Yeerks lower themselves to behaving like humans." He jerked his head. "Take her away."

The Hork-Bajir dragged the girl into the building. The older man handed the Rubbermaid to another human-Controller. "Too many of our people going host-happy. These human hosts can be insidious. Check this in with the contraband locker."

"They're running out of room over there. They've taken in over two hundred human pounds of this stuff."

Two hundred pounds?

"Well, hello opportunity," I whispered.

CHAPTER 25

They kept the oatmeal in more of a shack than a building. It was like one of those tin sheds that people put in their backyards to store rakes and hoses and the lawn mower.

However, it was guarded by four very alert, very serious-looking Hork-Bajir.

The shed was perhaps fifty feet from the edge of the Yeerk pool itself, and just behind the "human" cafeteria.

I took a deep breath. Okay. Marco was free, but I didn't know where. Jake, Tobias, and Ax were all prisoners, probably back in the security building. Cassie was somewhere, and I had no idea where or if she was okay. I had to stifle an urge to cry at the thought of Cassie hurt.

Okay, now stick to business, I told myself sharply. *You're the only one who can save them.*

In addition to everything else, I knew Visser Three was on his way, Jake and Tobias were running short of morphing time, and there were two hundred pounds of maple and ginger oatmeal sitting in a shed within fifty feet of the pool.

There had to be some way to make all this work. I just had to step back and see the big picture. Somehow. But the truth is, I'm not good at that kind of thing. Jake sees "big pictures." So does Cassie, in a different way. Me, I see what's right in front of me. I'm good at taking action.

Okay. First of all, whatever you're going to do, do it before Visser Three gets here.

First priority was rescuing my friends. I just needed time to —

ScrrrEEEET! ScrrrEEEET! ScrrrEEEET!

An alarm! Flashing lights! Hork-Bajir running. Running toward the store room where I'd Draconed those people.

Oh.

Okay, that was stupid. I should have realized they'd be found. Now the Yeerks would know they hadn't gotten all of us.

<One more time. It's me, Marco. Calling Rachel. Come on, Rachel. You're starting to worry us all now. Where are you?>

THUMP! BUMP! People rushing all around

137

me. Hurrying. A huge Taxxon slithered past, needle-legs flashing, its big red, round mouth gasping at the air.

What had Marco said? *You're starting to worry us all now?* Us *all*? Did that mean he'd contacted all the others?

Someone grabbed me. "What's the matter with you? Get to your action station! There are more Andalite scum among us!"

The man released me and ran about three feet. Then he stopped. I could practically see the wheels turning in his head. He turned back to me, his face alive with suspicion.

I stepped right up to him so no one would see the flash. I lifted the Dracon beam and squeezed the trigger.

TSEEEWWW!

"Ahhh!" The Dracon blast was too close. Some of the energy bounced back off the man and stunned me. It was like grabbing a bare electrical wire and jabbing it in my stomach. I clutched my stomach and backed away.

Heads turned. Eyes narrowed.

"He's one of them!" I yelled, pointing at the prostrate man. "He tried to shoot me with this!" I held up the Dracon beam as evidence.

A crowd rushed forward, Hork-Bajir among them. They encircled the man as I backed away and tried to become invisible.

ScrrrEEEET! ScrrrEEEET! ScrrrEEEET!

<Oh, Ra-chel,> Marco sang in my head. <Where are you?>

"Where's the girl who was just here?" I heard a voice yell from the midst of the crowd.

I turned and walked away. *Walk, don't run*, I told myself.

"Well, *find* her!"

"Rachel!" a voice hissed.

I swear I almost wet myself. I reached for the Dracon beam.

"It's just me."

Cassie! She was suddenly right there in front of me.

"Oh, man, am I glad to see you! How did you get here?"

"How did *you* get here?"

"Never mind," I said. "I'm in trouble."

"I am so *not* surprised," she said.

"Come on, we have to get away from here." We walked away and I filled her in on what I knew. Which wasn't much.

"So, what do we do?" she asked.

"I was hoping *you'd* have some ideas."

"Well, we'd better get Jake, Tobias, and Ax first."

"Yeah, but how? They're surrounded by Hork-Bajir on a high state of alert. Visser Three's on his way."

I saw her glance at the Yeerk pool. "They're almost helpless in their natural state, aren't they?"

Suddenly a loudspeaker crackled to life. A blastingly loud message in some language neither of us spoke. And then, to my amazement, the top of the dome began to open up. It was just a circle, and from the filtered quality of the light that came down I could tell it was the bottom of a tunnel. It must have cut straight through some portion of the bat cave.

Floating down on jets of brilliant blue gasses came a Bug fighter.

"Three guesses who that is," Cassie muttered.

CHAPTER 26

The Bug fighter bearing Visser Three floated down to a gentle landing not a hundred feet away.

I caught a glimpse of him as he stepped out. He looked like an older Ax. But even though Visser Three had infested an Andalite body, there was no mistaking him for a real Andalite. Not once you knew him. There was a darkness you couldn't see, but could definitely feel. A darkness spreading outward from him that caused people to lower their voices, speak in whispers, and try to shrink inside their own skin.

"Some butt is going to get kicked," I predicted.

The Visser's thought-speak roar filled every

brain in the Yeerk pool. <Seal every exit! No one move! Not a single twitch, do you hear me? I have secure troops coming down. Until they check you, no one moves. If any of you see any movement, destroy! Destroy it! Do you understand me? I will not tolerate failure!>

Two more Bug fighters were descending now. Visser Three was being careful. He knew we could be anyone. He knew we could even theoretically be in Hork-Bajir morph or Taxxon morph. He'd brought fresh Hork-Bajir down from his Blade ship to begin checking us, one by one.

"We're toast," Cassie said, barely moving her lips.

We were alongside the building used to feed human-Controllers. We were partly blocked from view, and almost everyone in the place was staring straight ahead at Visser Three.

Still, there were two human-Controllers and a Taxxon behind us, where they would see us if we moved.

"Into the cafeteria here," I whispered. "Combat mode. Get ready."

"Get ready for . . . where did you get *that*?"

Cassie had seen my Dracon beam as I drew it. I spun to face the Taxxon. "He moved! It's an AN-DALITE!" I screamed.

I squeezed the trigger.

TSEEEWWW! Down went the Taxxon like a sack of pudding.

TSEEEWWW! Down went the first human-Controller!

TSEEEWWW! Down went the second.

We were clear. For about three seconds. I ducked into the cafeteria and was already starting to morph. The building was empty. Everyone was outside, gaping in fear at their leader.

<Who's firing over there?> the Visser bellowed. <I said, freeze!>

Cassie and I banged through folding chairs and slammed around tables loaded with interrupted meals.

"Back there!" I yelled, pointing to a door. I yanked it open. A food pantry.

And there, sitting calmly atop a crate of canned minestrone and enjoying a banana, sat a gorilla.

"Marco?"

<No, some *other* gorilla,> he said. <I've been trying to contact you two for —>

"Some other time!" I yelled. "Hold this! I'm morphing!" I tossed him the Dracon beam.

<Cool!>

"Visser Three is here. Jake, Tobias, and Ax are surrounded by Hork-Bajir, and there are two hundred pounds of oatmeal in a shed!"

The gorilla blinked. <You have some brilliant yet probably suicidal idea, Xena?>

"No."

<What are you morphing?>

"Grizzly bear. It's butt-kicking time!"

"No, wait!" Cassie said. "The stupid oatmeal! That's the key. If that was in the pool, they'd all go nuts. At least it would be a huge distraction."

"We have to get out the front door of this place, around the building, back to the shed where they store it. A long way."

Marco nodded, like a wise gorilla. <Doesn't that mean it's right back here?> He pointed through the wall.

I smiled. "Come to think of it, it would be a lot shorter trip if we went *through* the wall."

"Through the wall. Then through the two Hork-Bajir guarding the oatmeal. Then what?" Cassie asked.

"Then . . ." I began. I sighed. "I don't know."

<Good plan,> Marco said.

"Let's —" I began.

Marco held up one massive, leathery paw. <No, no. My turn,> he said. <All right, let's do it!>

CHAPTER 27

I began to morph the grizzly bear. But then I stopped. We needed raw power. Truck-style power.

"You guys may get a little cramped," I warned. "I'm gonna get big."

I began to morph the elephant.

It's funny with morphing. It's like choosing your weapons in an old-time duel. In the old days two guys would insult each other, then they would arrange through their friends to "settle" the matter. The person who was challenged would get his choice of weapons. They'd go off early one morning, very civilized, with all the proper ceremony, and sword fight or shoot each other.

Pretty much like some people do today, only nowadays the duelists always seem to slaughter some innocent bystanders.

But that's a little of what it's like. I was going into battle. Which weapon should I use? I liked the bear because it was so utterly powerful and destructive. But in this case, the elephant morph was the proper weapon. And just like with one of those old-time, early-morning duels, I had plenty of time to think about being scared.

I began to change. I began to get large. My legs thickened to become telephone poles. My arms thickened even more and the weight of them made me fall forward.

My fingers and toes disappeared, leaving behind only thick, bony nails. I realized I could see something flapping around my head. Flapping like someone shaking a sheet out of the dryer. It was my ears, growing thin and huge.

My face bulged outward. It was as if someone were blowing my head up like a balloon. My eyes moved apart, spreading farther and farther, blurring my vision. My nose melted with my upper lip and began to grow like some nightmare Pinocchio. It grew till it wasn't a nose anymore, but a rope, a cable, a massive octopus tentacle so strong I could rip trees out of the ground.

I was monstrous, towering huge above Marco, and Cassie in her wolf morph. My back pressed against the roof. My sides shoved crates and boxes aside.

<Marco, look out!> I yelled and Marco dropped the Dracon beam trying to get out of the way. Because at that moment, my teeth ground and cracked and suddenly sprouted. Out, out, out from my mouth they grew, forming two long, curved tusks.

If Marco had stayed where he was, he'd have been impaled.

<Marco, get the Dracon beam. You dropped it. Your fingers are the only ones that can work it.>

<Dropped it where? Under you? Great.> He crawled awkwardly beneath my bulging gray stomach and emerged with the Dracon beam in his fist.

<Okay,> I said. <Right for the oatmeal shed, no stopping. Ready?>

<Ready,> Cassie said.

<You know, Jake was right. You just never hear about oatmeal being involved in any of the great battles of history,> Marco observed.

<Yeah, whatever,> I said tersely. <Come on.>

I didn't have to do much to go through the back wall of the pantry we were in. I just leaned forward and pushed my head against the wall. My head alone weighed more than half a ton. It was a serious battering ram.

Crrrrr-UNCH! Crunch! Scree-UNCH!

Down came the wall. Down came half the roof on my back. Out we barreled, an elephant, a wolf, and a lumbering gorilla.

The shed was thirty feet away. No more. Not even two body lengths for me. One, two, three steps and I was there!

The two Hork-Bajir yelled and almost ran, but then held their ground. I had to admire that. Go to the zoo some time. Take a good, long look at an African elephant, and imagine that thing charging for you. See how long you'd want to stand there.

SLASH!

A lightning-quick swipe with an arm blade, and I had a bright red line in my trunk. It was just a shallow cut, but it hurt.

"HhhhrrrooooooREEEE-Unh!" I screamed.

I kept my speed, and plowed straight into the Hork-Bajir. Ten thousand pounds of fast-moving elephant.

The brave Hork-Bajir-Controller was out of the fight.

No time to stop. I saw Marco and Cassie take down the other Hork-Bajir.

<Two more Hork-Bajir coming!> Cassie yelled.

I backed up a few feet and slammed forward. I hit the shed with my head.

WHAM!

The four walls of the shed literally blew outward. Like someone had set off a bomb inside it. The walls burst outward from the impact. The roof fell and then slid aside.

A blue barrel, like a beer keg, rolled away. A piece of debris stopped it. There were five other barrels, all standing there in a group.

<The oatmeal!> I said.

<The instant maple and ginger oatmeal!> Marco corrected gleefully.

<Get them!> a huge, thought-speak voice roared. The voice of Visser Three.

I turned my head to look. An entire army of Hork-Bajir, Taxxons, and human-Controllers was rushing for us. There was no way out. No way at all.

And there, in the midst of the onrushing army, was Visser Three.

I wrapped my trunk around one of the barrels of confiscated oatmeal. I lifted it up like a feather. I saw the closest Hork-Bajir hesitate.

I threw the barrel in a high arc. It landed with a big, soggy splash, right in the middle of the Yeerk pool.

<It's not sinking!> Cassie cried.

<Marco. Point the Dracon beam at the barrel. Now.>

The big gorilla raised his mighty arm and aimed the Dracon beam at the barrel.

<Your move, Visser,> I said.

CHAPTER 28

<Stop!> that awful voice roared.

And every living thing stopped. They barely breathed. Hork-Bajir stood poised as if they'd been frozen. When the Visser said "stop," you stopped. Period.

He came forward, pushing human and Hork-Bajir and Taxxon aside. He came forward till nothing separated him from us except a shield of three straining, awkwardly frozen Hork-Bajir and a twitching Taxxon.

His Andalite stalk eyes swept from side to side, sizing up the situation. His main eyes looked right at me.

<There's nothing in that barrel but garbage.>

<Then you won't mind if my friend fires and blows it up.>

It was always deadly dangerous talking to Visser Three. In addition to an Andalite's body, he had an Andalite mind under his evil control. He might figure out that I was not an Andalite in morph, but a human.

He laughed. Not a nice laugh.<There are perhaps a thousand Yeerks in that pool. The . . . the product in that barrel might affect half of them before we could get it cleared up. Five hundred Yeerks.>

He paused to consider. <And against that, I suppose you want your fellow terrorists released and a chance to escape.>

<Exactly,> I said.

Marco still held the Dracon beam aimed at the wallowing barrel.

<Then I'd better give you my answer,> Visser Three said with silky menace.

Before he could say it, I knew. I'd seen it in his eyes. In his body language.

He was writing off five hundred of his own people. Condemning them to madness. He didn't care. It would be a setback, but that was all. Beyond that, he didn't care.

Visser Three cared for nothing.

Oh, wait. Visser Three *did* care about one thing.

No time to think. No time to plan. I surged forward suddenly, just as Visser Three was saying, <Destroy them —>

I surged my five tons forward, trunk outstretched.

Visser Three leaped back. Right into a Taxxon who was following orders by freezing.

I plowed through the Hork-Bajir and reached for the Visser. My trunk went around his upper body.

FWAPP! His Andalite tail slashed!

Miss!

I squeezed my trunk, flexed the muscles in my neck and shoulders, and up went the Visser. I yanked him up off the ground.

FWAPP! He slashed again, and this time I bellowed in pain. The blade had hit the side of my face. It nearly cut right through one eye. The agony was unbearable.

But I couldn't hesitate.

I lifted the Visser high in the air. I heaved him, just as he slashed again.

Through the air he flew.

PAH-LOOOSH!

Visser Three hit the Yeerk pool.

I was reeling in pain. Pain like nothing I'd ever imagined.

<Oh, no, Rachel!> Cassie cried.

I ignored her. No time for pain. No time. I had

to play this out. Fortunately, I know just a little about Andalite physiology. See, they eat and drink through their hooves. Right now the Visser was absorbing the water of the Yeerk pool.

I glared with my one remaining eye at the Visser, floundering in the pool.

<*Now* do you care if we blow up that barrel?> I asked him. <Now do you care?>

CHAPTER 29

It turned out yes, yes, he cared. Visser Three would sacrifice hundreds of his fellow Yeerks to the oatmeal madness. After all, it was war, and sacrifices had to be made sometimes.

But those sacrifices obviously did not include him.

I kicked the rest of the barrels into the pool, just so Marco couldn't possibly miss. Then Cassie went off to free the others. The Hork-Bajir, the Taxxons, and the human-Controllers were still busy being very, very still. If any of them had shown initiative, they could have probably taken us out. They might well have been able to get Marco before he could hit one of the barrels.

But you know what? Terrified underlings never

show initiative. The Yeerks there may have hated us. But they were terrified of Visser Three.

We freed Jake, Tobias, and Ax. Then we headed, very carefully, for one of the exits. We climbed the stairs backward, with Marco pointing the Dracon beam the whole way up.

Only because of Tobias did we see what happened next. Hidden behind my massive, pain-wracked bulk, he demorphed. Halfway up that interminable stairway, he resumed hawk shape. And it was his hawk vision that saw.

<He's morphing! The Visser. He's halfway morphed!>

<He's getting out of his Andalite shape, taking on some form that won't absorb the water,> Jake said. <Then the stupid oatmeal won't bother him. He'll come for us!>

<How far along is he?> Ax demanded.

<Can't tell,> Tobias cried. <He's going under! He's submerging!>

I glanced up the stairs. A long way still to go. And I was weak from my injuries. Yet I couldn't demorph and reveal that my true shape was human. Plenty of time for Visser Three to come popping up out of the water in one of his vile, alien morphs and come for us.

We were weak and exposed on the stairs. I was practically out of the fight. Jake was still a bat. No way to win if he managed to come after us.

<Marco has to shoot,> I said. I looked at Cassie and Tobias to see if either of them would object.

<He's not leaving us any choice,> Tobias said grimly. He hopped over to sit on Marco's shoulder. <You're aiming high,> he said. <A hair lower. Lower . . . fire!>

TSEEEWWW!

Far down below us, one of the floating barrels went, POOMPF!

A gray substance like confetti exploded out and settled in the water.

<That should keep them busy,> Tobias said. <Let's bail!>

It was pandemonium down in the Yeerk pool. Hork-Bajir and humans and Taxxons all rushing around, trying to haul their Visser out of the water. Trying to scoop up the madness-inducing oatmeal before it could dissolve completely.

Then I fell over. I didn't waver or stagger. I just fell over. Five tons of sagging elephant flesh splayed out across a dozen stone steps.

<Demorph!> Jake yelled at once.

Cassie rushed over, helpless to do much with her wolf paws. <It's the loss of blood! She's passing out. Rachel, you have to demorph.>

<He's up!> Tobias yelled. <He's out of the water. Oh, man! What the . . . Ax, what is that thing?>

<I don't know,> Ax admitted. <It's no creature I've ever seen before. But it looks extremely dangerous.>

I was demorphing as fast as I could. <You guys get going! I'll catch up!>

<Yeah, right, Rachel,> Cassie said.

<It's like some kind of pterodactyl almost,> Jake said. <Like one of those flying dinosaurs. Only it's covered in quills all over its back.>

Jake was demorphing. I was demorphing. Too slowly.

<All we have is a monkey and a wolf!> I yelled. <You guys run! You can pick up Jake and run!>

<A monkey?> Marco said archly. <You know, I almost could run off and leave you.>

<You have more than a gorilla and a wolf,> Ax said calmly. <You have an Andalite.>

I was shrinking all the while. And as I became less elephant and more human, the pain began to diminish. I could feel strength returning. But I was still so tired. Could I morph again?

<I have to report there are Hork-Bajir coming down the stairs toward us,> Ax said. He was the only one of us who'd been looking in that direction. It helped to have four eyes.

"Great," Jake snapped, human again. "We're trapped. And here he comes!"

I turned my now-human head toward the

sound of vast, leathery wings. I saw something that might have been a winged porcupine, only the quills were each five feet long. Its head was elongated forward and back. The beak itself was another five feet.

It flew slowly, with great effort, but it was coming closer. My heart sank. Had he seen us in our human bodies?

I turned my head to look back up the stairs. The Hork-Bajir were a hundred feet away, pounding down on us. We were trapped. No time to morph, even. Trapped!

The stairway entered solid rock and earth just ten feet upward. The Visser's monster wouldn't be able to fly in there. But if we ascended that far, we'd run right into the Hork-Bajir.

I looked to Cassie, my best friend. I guess I wanted to say something meaningful.

And that's when it hit me. "Give me the Dracon beam!"

"It's not gonna stop that . . . that *thing*! It's armored all over. Nothing will stop that thing."

I didn't have time to argue. I snatched the Dracon beam from Marco. I turned and plowed up the stairs, right for the Hork-Bajir.

"Follow me!"

"But —"

"Just come on!"

Up we ran. The distance between us and the

Hork-Bajir closed at a startling rate. The monster was coming on fast.

"Everyone down! Cover your heads! Mole!" I screamed. "MOLE!" And I raised the Dracon beam straight up. Aimed it at point-blank range right up at the hanging rock and dirt roof.

I thumbed the power switch and squeezed the trigger.

And the entire world fell down on me.

CHAPTER 30

I wasn't crushed by a rock. I was glad for that. I was smashed and banged up pretty good. And oh, was I scared.

Buried alive!

It had actually happened. I'd even made it happen. Buried alive under rock and dirt and struggling Hork-Bajir.

But what can you do when you're buried alive? You can either sit there screaming in blind, idiot panic. Or you can dig your way out. At least, if you're a mole you can.

I was worried about Cassie and Marco. They'd both still been in morph, so they had an extra phase to pass through before they could become moles again.

But wolves and gorillas aren't easy to kill. We all morphed and dug our lonely tunnels upward.

It took a long time. I had to stop and hollow out enough space to demorph to human so I didn't end up trapped in mole morph. Talk about wanting to scream.

But on the second round I emerged into the bat cave.

It took another hour for all of us to get there. We'd meet up in the absolute darkness, one by one, then in a small, edgy, worried group.

Tobias was the last to arrive.

"You scared us to death! Where have you been?" I yelled at him.

<I was worried about you, too, Rachel,> he said, with a smile in his silent voice.

Finally we morphed into our bat shapes. Exhausted beyond all belief. I could have just lain down there in the eternal darkness and slept for a week.

And then, just as we were echolocating around, looking for the exit, the strangest thing happened. The entire cave came alive.

In a slow-motion rush all the bats began to drop their grip on the rock roof. They dropped, opened their wings, fired their echolocation sounds, and took off.

<Must be sundown,> Cassie said.

<Yeah, but sundown of which day?> I muttered.

We exploded from the cave. Maybe a hundred thousand bats. Maybe a million. Who can count that many bats?

We headed for home, too exhausted even to make dumb jokes or laugh or be happy we had survived.

But as tired as I was, there was one thing I wanted to do.

Maybe I have a soft spot for lunatics. After all, if I ever told anyone what my life was like, I'd be in a rubber room so fast I'd get whiplash.

When I was done, I flew home and demorphed in my room.

I went downstairs as calmly as if I'd never left.

"Where EXACTLY have you been all day, young lady?" my mother demanded.

But just then the phone rang. My mom took the call. She listened and kept saying, "What?" She said "what?" about nine times, each time louder than the time before.

Then she sat down and stared at Sarah and Jordan and me.

"What is it?" I asked.

"It's my client. Poor Mr. Edelman." She shook her head like she was trying to clear something away. "He escaped from the institution."

"The nuthouse?" Jordan asked.

"He's gone. Ran away. But what's bizarre is how it happened. They're claiming a grizzly bear

162

calmly walked in, knocked the doors down, and told the man . . . in some kind of psychic way . . . I mean, you have to envision a *talking* grizzly bear . . . a *psychic* talking bear . . . told the man . . ." She checked the notes she'd written down. "Told him to leave, get out, but not to do anything dumb like trying to hurt himself because . . . the bear . . . had had a really lousy day and didn't want to have to save him again."

Jordan and Sarah stared at my mother like she was crazy.

"Hey, I'm not the one who claims to have seen all this," my mother said defensively.

I shrugged. "Bunch of nuts," I said dismissively. "I mean, come on. A grizzly bear. Right."

It wasn't much. I couldn't really help Mr. Edelman. No one could. But some of the time his own, human mind was in charge. And during those times, in between the mad ravings of the Yeerk, I wanted him to be free.

The doorbell rang.

"It's MAR-co," Jordan sang. She thinks he's cute.

"Tell him to go away," I yelled back. "I'm tired."

Jordan reappeared a few moments later. She was carrying a huge stack of small boxes. "Your friend MAR-co says his dad is making him get rid of all this stuff."

She dumped the boxes of maple and ginger oatmeal all over the kitchen table.

That was the end of the first and only great battle ever to involve oatmeal.

And, by the way, if you ever see some poor, mad, deranged gentleman wandering the streets and raving away about things that live in his head . . . well, if you can handle it, give the man your spare change.

#18 The Decision

$\mathbf{I}$ am very good at passing for human, if I say so myself. I have learned the customs and habits perfectly so that I seem entirely normal.

That's how I am able to pass in even the most human of places. For example, the mall. . . .

The mall also houses the most wonderful eating places. . . .

Taste is very, very powerful.

I was wearing artificial skin and artificial hooves like a human. I approached the counter of my very favorite eating place.

"Hello," I said, making mouth sounds with my human mouth. "I will work for money. Muh-nee. Mnee. . . ."

"Do you want to order something?" the human said to me.

"I require money so that I may exchange it for the delicious cinnamon buns." I explained. "Bun-zuh."

"I'll get the manager."

"Bun-zuh," I said. I find the "z" sound especially enjoyable. It tickles the mouth parts. . . .

The manager came and I explained my re-
quest to her.

"Well, I can't give you a job," she said. "I
think you're under age. But I guess if you're hungry I could have you clear some of those tables
and give you some food."

This was acceptable to me.

"Poor kid," she said to the other human as I
turned away. "A little off in the head, maybe. But
a good-looking boy."

I soon discovered what she meant by clearing
tables. In this part of the mall there are many
tables, surrounded by eating places. The tables
were littered with delicious things!

On the first table I found thin, crisp, salty-
greasy triangles covered with a bright yellow se-
cretion. I ate them and they were very good. . . .

Then at last, I saw what I wanted. Two large,
steaming hot, glistening cinnamon buns. Two humans were sitting very near the cinnamon buns.

They were going to eat my buns!

I raced over as quickly as my wobbly human
legs could go. "I am clearing these tables!" I
cried.

The humans looked at me. "We haven't eaten
yet."

"Good," I said, relieved. I grabbed the two cinnamon buns and carried them away.

"Hey! Hey, stop!"

I began to shove the first bun into my mouth. . . .

"What are you doing?" the manager cried as she came running over.

"I amm glearing khe khables," I said. It is very difficult to speak while eating. Just one of the many design flaws in humans. . . .

She pulled me away, causing me to drop a small portion of them from my mouth. . . .

"Okay, now look, son, if you're that desperate for food, there's a tray of buns here that are just a bit stale. You can help yourself. You poor kid."

"For me?" I asked in a voice choked with emotion.

"Sure, son. Go ahead and have one."

Let me make one final point here: human mouth-sound language is very fuzzy at times. "Have one," she'd said.

One mouthful? One bun?

One tray?

It was certainly not my fault if there was any confusion.

You are about to enter Zero-space...

ANIMORPHS

Mosquitoes seem like the perfect creatures to morph. They're small. Small enough to slip by unsuspecting Yeerks. But big enough to cause a huge problem. For Ax, this means a chance to return to his own people. For the Animorphs, it means there may be no way to get back to Earth. Ever.

ANIMORPHS #18: THE DECISION

COMING IN APRIL!

K.A. Applegate